D1106001

NORTH

A NOVEL

By Roy Robbins

NOVEL
North

POETRY
Poster Art Nights

PLAYS
Prove That You Love Me
Slow Instructions
Sudden Improvement
King Momo

NORTH

A NOVEL

*For the Stimperts,
with Thanks,*

Roy Robbins

ROY

and from

ROBBINS

*Susan
with great
thanks!*

BEACH GLASS
BOOKS

BEACH GLASS
BOOKS

A portion of this book previously was published in slightly different form in the *Main Street Rag* literary magazine, Charlotte, North Carolina.

Published by Beach Glass Books.
First printing May 2020

ISBN 978-0-9987881-8-0

Manufactured in the United States of America. All paper suppliers hold PEFC, SFI and FSC certifications assuring their support of responsible forest management.

Cover image by Unholy Vault Designs
Author photo courtesy of the Earl Hamner Jr. Theater
Jacket and book design by Ray McAllister

Library of Congress Cataloging-in-Publication Data applied for
Robbins, Roy, 1939–
North: A Novel / by Roy Robbins

Library of Congress Control Number: 2020934334

Beach Glass Books
BeachGlassBooks.com

FOR OLIVER, COURTNEY, THOMAS,
REMI AND LULU

PUBLISHER'S NOTE

We never thought we would publish a book like this. By that, we mean a novel. A work of fiction. A work of literary fiction.

Beach Glass Books' catalogue is replete with historical books and coastal books, with collections of essays and columns, with stories of true crime and even a child's suicide. Award-winners, most, but non-fiction, all. With the exception of children's books, we have never ventured into fiction nor intended to.

And then we saw *North*.

North is a murder mystery. But below, it is a story of power and corruption, of family and love and pain, of turning a blind eye, of coming to terms. The themes are Faulknerian, and so is the setting, and, not to push this analogy too far, the writing is compelling. That Roy Robbins is an award-winning playwright and a poet—who else, after all, would pull a chapter title from a 19th century poem?—is not surprising. He writes like a master. How is it this is only his first novel? We don't know, but are glad it ended up here. We think you will be glad it has ended up in your hands.

And, no, we may never publish a novel again.

There aren't many like *North*.

Ray McAllister
Beach Glass Books

NORTH

ONE

The Knife in the Wall

There are many small towns in north Florida that resemble each other, as if one person using a single plan had laid them out. I had never really noticed this lack of variation before, until, a couple of years after my wife Marty left me, and I returned home for what would be the two funerals.

My brother Jess had called with the news that Mom was really sick, and my therapist, Dr. Cranston advised me to go home and talk to her before it was too late. "Think about your mother and the people you grew up with if you want to know why you kept trying to kill yourself. Go back to your hometown and find out what kind of woman brought you into the world." It seemed like good advice. The problem is I can't casually say in a conversation that my doctor has diagnosed me as seriously suicidal. People start edging away from you and then very quickly excuse themselves. When that happens, my mind still goes blank and I get a vacant look in my eyes, as if a barrier of some kind was preventing me from thinking about my family and North and the people I knew there.

So I came back to Florida to find my mother, that is, to understand her by taking Dr. Cranston's advice, but I waited an extra week to clear up some things at work, and mother would lose consciousness and be moved into an intensive care unit before I could talk to her. She died the week before someone killed Leon Putnam with a single blow to the head. So I inadvertently reached North and home between the two funerals, the one that I missed for my mother and the second one for Leon. I never thought of the two deaths together until Dr. Cranston suggested that they might be connected.

When I was growing up, many of the small towns like North had a road of fine sand that ran parallel to the main highway; in my town, this road was called Putnam's Track. A church stood sentinel at each end, guarding the junctions where the white sand curved back to join the black asphalt. Putnam's Store and the Post Office sat across from each other, equidistant between the two churches and flanked by several old homes that were almost hidden among the enormous live oaks. A few abandoned buildings still line both sides of the highway. Putnam's Store is gone now, and the old homes and churches are empty, collapsing into themselves like rotten fruit; only the Post Office remains, attached at one end to the back wall of a gas station. The town's name, North, is the cause of the joke we always heard from strangers passing through and stopping for gas: "North of what?"

North's only claim to fame is for being the home of

Leon Putnam, the man who served the longest term as Speaker of Florida's House of Representatives. He was often referred to as "The First Man," not just because of his wealth, but because whenever something new came along, he was the first man in the county to try it.

Before he was murdered, Leon made arrangements to be buried above ground, hoping, we supposed, to keep his body from being dissolved by the spring waters that flow from all directions through the porous, sandy soil. Leon was buried over his wife, Edna, since he had not bothered to arrange a place for her beside him in the crypt. They had married early, and had one daughter, Laurel, before Edna called it quits, we heard. They never divorced, and after her mother died, Laurel inherited everything, although Leon's several mistresses, black and white, spent a lot of his money for him before he was killed.

My name is Jonathan Hallam Parker. Everyone in North calls me Hal, except my brother Jess, who sometimes, in private, calls me Bump, because when I was just turning four, I had an enormous, misshapen toy truck that I pulled behind me across the wooden floors of our old-fashioned country house. As heavy as a bowling ball, it banged along behind me making loud ka-thumps. My brother, Jess, six years older, and a perfectionist even then, was starting the fifth grade. My percussion drove him crazy, which also made me happy.

One morning as I bumped in for breakfast with my truck, Jess unexpectedly stood up at the kitchen table and screamed, "Here he comes again, damn it! Bump! Bump! Bump!" Then, as I sat down next to Mama, he snatched up a butcher knife and hurled it at me. It was a good throw, but missed me. The knife whizzed past my head and buried itself in the wall.

I sat watching Mama as she stared at Jess, who was inching down into his seat gripping the corners of the table, looking at Mama like a rabbit trying to decide which way to run before, as my granddaddy would say, the big hawk lit.

Mama walked over to Jess, reached out and began moving his plate away from him, then picked it up and broke it over his head in one perfect blow, the eggs and grits sliding down his neck. Jess sat hunched over in a frozen posture as if changed to stone, not flinching. The knife stayed in the wall for months, and like the knife, the name Hal stuck. I never saw Mama act that way again, deliberately violent. It was shocking to feel her cold fury come up out of her.

Later, after the two funerals, I would often think of Mama in her watery grave, not above ground like the expensive one of Leon's, and I wonder if she is waiting for me down there. I know how crazy this sounds, like some old ballad, but it is what it is. And I wonder if Leon's spirit, flaming past her in the darkness, called out to her after he died. I hope not. I know that he might have thought she would try to intercede on his behalf. She had that angelic face, but she broke the plate over Jess' head, and her other son is "suicide prone." That's why I was back in North. "Going south to North," I told Dr. Cranston, who said, "It's not a joke. Go back and try to find out some answers. Telling a joke just deflects you from finding out about what happened to you as a child."

The mystery in North is still who killed Leon, and I hope that it will be possible for me to uncover some of the mystery about why he was killed, and why I wanted to kill him myself. After his stroke, his daughter, Laurel, had arranged for someone to take care of Leon at home. His mind was clear, and I heard that he could sit in a chair and watch television, but when he tried to talk, words would come out that were all vowels, and during visits, he would grow more and more frantic as he tried to make people understand him, gesturing feebly with a desperate expression on his face until he was almost howling, "Eyaa Wineznn Ommm Oneee!"

Now, back in North, I decided that I ought to visit Laurel and the nurse she had hired. I wanted to talk about the murder and maybe about my mother, though that would be difficult—I knew some of the truth about my mother and Leon and I didn't know what his daughter Laurel thought, if anything, beyond the fact that we had been neighbors. In fact, we had been more than neighbors; Leon was the banker who foreclosed on my dad's orange groves.

I forced myself to drive down to where Putnam's store used to be, and take the turn that led to Leon's house. Laurel had built a house on the lot next to Leon's, and the lot on the other side of Leon's was where the neighbor, Mrs. Johnson, lived. I tried Mrs. Johnson's house first. There was no answer when I knocked on the door, and after waiting in the yard for thirty minutes, I left and drove over to Leon's house, on the off chance that Laurel might show up. While I waited, I tried to put together what I knew about Leon's murder.

I had heard that Laurel had taken a degree in library science and was working in what Jess called the rare book department at the University library in Gainesville. Laurel, Jess said, spent more time working on Leon's papers and accounts than she spent on her university job, but since she was Leon's daughter, no one at the library ever said anything. Laurel was smart, like Leon, and I was sure she was more than just Leon's secretary; dealing with rare papers and manuscripts at the library would give her the training in how to organize Leon's papers. But I wondered how much of Leon's affairs she knew about? Did she see Leon's secret financial records, about the lives broken, the blackmail payments, the mortgages foreclosed on, and the money spent on mistresses, with their housing and upkeep, or, more likely, did she see only the official public documents about the legislative Leon, the Leon who decreed what laws passed, who made speeches and handed out political favors?

The coroner's report said that Leon had been killed less than an hour after his nurse, Joyce Goodman, left for Palatka to have some of Leon's prescriptions filled. When questioned, she said that she always arranged for a neighbor, a Mrs. Johnson, to look in on Leon, but something happened the day Leon was murdered, and Mrs. Johnson never came. Leon's nurse claimed that she often left Leon for a couple of hours or so, and that the doctor had approved it. The police reported that the neighbor, Mrs. Johnson, had said she would look out her window to see if the nurse's car was missing before walking over to stay with Leon. But this time she did not see the car leave, and so had thought that the nurse, Mrs. Goodman, was still at Leon's. Laurel says that her instructions were that her father was never to be left alone. Laurel, the report continued, said that the doctor had never approved of the arrangement between the nurse and Mrs. Johnson, and that her instructions were to never leave Leon alone.

Leon's nurse had left the back door unlocked for the neighbor while she was in Palatka. During her absence, someone (or maybe more than one person) came in and killed Leon. As far as Laurel could tell, nothing had been stolen. When the nurse came back, Leon was sitting in his chair, dead from one blow to the head, not from behind, but a dead center blow to his forehead.

I waited for Laurel to come home, but she never did. The next day I came back, just before the above ground funeral for Leon, but Laurel had already left for the church. I had a couple of hours to kill before the funeral service would start, and so I stood on the dock behind Leon's house, watching a diver as he bobbed up to the surface of the lake, searching for whatever it was someone might have used to bash Leon's head in. No one else was there except John Moses, the county sheriff. After about thirty minutes of watching, he saw the diver come up and shake his head. Sheriff Moses asked if I would stay "just in case the diver found something," while he went back to town. In another half hour I was on the dock alone, while the diver drove away with nothing to show for his work except two empty air tanks. The lake was calm, and I remembered that I was standing near the place where, as a boy, I had watched Leon trying to rape Nancy Ebersole, a friend and classmate of Laurel's and my brother Jess.

I hadn't thought about that for a long time, and then, standing on the dock, I looked down into the water where it had happened, and it was like a dream; I was eleven again, swimming underwater with a diver's mask on while I looked for big bass hiding in the dark spaces around the edges of the sawgrass near the dock. There were cottonmouths and a gator or two in the lake, but Jess and I swam in it anyway. Mama never asked us if we had seen a snake.

I could see Nancy Ebersole as she swam in slow, graceful circles around some boats Leon had tied up. For whatever reason, Nancy had taken a break from the graduation party. Maybe she wanted to wash off some of the smoke from the fire. Of course, she knew I was there and would be looking at her in her white bathing suit, and could see her legs kicking and her beautiful breasts arching just below the surface as her arms reached out in slow, steady strokes.

It was getting dark, and I knew that in another five minutes or so I would have to go up to the house and watch television, while the serious couples settled down underneath the blankets scattered around the fire.

Then, out of nowhere there was a sound in the water of someone wading out along the dock, someone very big whose legs moved through the water with slow, powerful thrusts. I guessed it was Nancy's boyfriend Ed Willis, and I knew I had better not be caught underwater staring at Nancy, so I came up for a little gasp of air and kept moving, gliding through the darkening water as the sawgrass clicked around me.

The next thing I knew there was a muffled scream from Nancy, and I whipped around and swam underwater back toward the dock. As I came closer, I could see the legs and large belly of a man, standing on the sandy bottom of the lake. Nancy was pinned up against one of the heavy black pilings that anchored the dock. She was just out of her depth, unable to gain a foothold, kicking helplessly as Leon (I knew immediately then who it was) pushed her harder and harder against the post. He had his body wedged between her legs, and I could see her bathing suit dangling down around her ankles. Leon's left arm went up out of the water, and I knew he must have been holding her by the throat. His other hand was working between her legs.

I had never seen any woman naked, and was so astonished that I tried to take a breath. I gagged, and came up with a loud, sucking gasp about ten feet behind Leon. Leon let go of Nancy and turned and looked at me and then up at the campfire. He gave a low snarl. "Where in hell did you come from?" and then slowly dog-paddled over to his boat and hauled himself up and over the side, then pushed the boat away from the dock, cranked the engine and roared out onto the lake. I turned to look for Nancy, but by now she had her bathing suit back on and was running down the dock toward the fire. One of her girlfriends was walking toward the lake, and she started running toward Nancy, and grabbed her by the shoulders so she had to stop. They leaned against each other while Nancy talked, and then I could see the other girl's head suddenly jerk and look out toward the dock. But Leon was gone. Arms around each other, they moved toward some lawn chairs at the edge of the lake. I watched as up by the fire, Jess lay down next to Laurel and pulled the blanket over them.

Then that memory faded, and I was standing on the dock with the diver gone and the sun blinding my eyes. For some reason, I felt as if someone else were nearby. Then I saw a woman on the next dock down the lake, a few hundred yards away. She was alone, and seemed to be staring at me, and I wondered if she were the neighbor who had failed to come over the day Leon was killed, and then, for some reason, I remembered that Nancy's mother, Sarah Ebersole, and my mother had all grown up together, and had remained good friends.

I waved to the woman on the dock and started toward Leon's house. Standing on the porch was a state trooper in full uniform. I looked at him sideways as I walked toward my car. He was a large man, wearing aviator sunglasses, watching the lake with no expression on his weathered face. How long had he been standing there, I wondered. Was he guarding the house? Leon, I guessed, was important enough for that. Probably Laurel had called the governor and requested that someone be posted at the house while she was away for the funeral service.

It was past noon, and so far, I didn't know anything more than I ever had. We all knew something about Leon, different and terrible things, except for Laurel maybe, and in some strange way Leon was the only thing I had in common with North or my mother. Jess had long since moved away and we were hardly in touch. During Leon's long life he had tormented, rewarded, ruined and humiliated most of us in an impartial way that ignored our small-town connections. Leon didn't really care about who you were; if you got in his way, he ruined you. If you moved aside, he didn't notice, and most people soon learned that not to be noticed by Leon was the best thing that could happen.

Leon's above ground funeral service was being held at the New Baptism Church and Campground on two miles outside North. A local minister named John Stickles had started it years ago. Back then it was a camp for young adults, as they said in Sunday school, and when Jess and his friends were in the tenth grade, we had started attending the services just to meet girls. We had all been 'saved' there four or five times, finding out that was the best way to get girls to notice us. At the end of the service, those who had given their lives to Christ went forward and held hands in a circle. Somehow Jess and his friends usually managed to end up holding the hands of the pretty girls. The camp survived for years in a few unpainted barrack-like buildings.

Reverend Stickles was a foolish man who often lost his focus as he strained to describe the wonders of the true way, and Jess and his friends had a favorite sermon they called The Teabag of Life, and it began by Reverend Stickles intoning "All of you have seen what happens when you put a teabag in a cup of hot water. JUST THINK ABOUT IT! That little bag begins to stain the clear water, until the water has . . . (A long pause here) . . . TURNED BROWN! Well, fellow sinners, that is what happens with THE WORD! Somehow, without noticing it, God's Word penetrates our lives and changes us forever, because Jeesuus . . . (another long pause) . . . is THE TEABAG OF LIFE!"

I arrived early for the funeral, so I could see the church fill up. Later, we would move outdoors for the graveside service where Leon would be buried above ground. Television crews were out on the road, but were stopped from coming on the grounds. Inside, there was an air of charged excitement and curiosity. Of course, they were trying to find out the latest news on the murder investigation. Half the benches had been roped off for all the dignitaries. Laurel, still unmarried, would be alone. One surviving aunt, her Aunt Janet, Edna's sister, was the only family. Leon had grown up in a foster home and had no family.

The church pews had filled, and people began standing along the walls, out into the foyer, and finally they lined up outside, in front of the steps. The governor was on his way from the airport in Gainesville with a police escort. Someone whispered there had been a big break in the investigation. Jess came in alone but didn't see me. His divorce was final last year. As everybody in North knew, Jess had never loved anyone but Laurel, and Laurel had always loved Jess. What stood between them was Leon, and now Leon was dead.

My mother never talked about the loss of the orange grove that had been in my father's family for three generations, but from what I could tell, my dad was one of the few people to stand up to Leon and mean it. When Leon said he was going to take our farm, Daddy said if Leon tried that, he would shoot him. We needed, I remember, an extension on our loan. But Leon pushed too hard, and we lost the groves. Daddy died from lung cancer the next year, and later, Leon had the stroke. You might say Leon Putnam ruined our family.

For some reason, I felt compelled to go to Leon's funeral. When I called Jess to tell him I was coming home, he told me all the details about how Leon died. He had been murdered in his own home, the door left unlocked, while his daughter, the neighbors, and the nurse were conveniently elsewhere.

As we waited in the church for the service to begin, a

few late arrivals straggled in. Mutt Cox came in a wheelchair, pushed by his wife Ann. Mutt was a short, heavy man with broad shoulders who had given Leon his start in the timber business, but who then lost everything when Leon put the squeeze on most of the landowners, underbidding Mutt and ruining him, and so Mutt, I was sure, had come to gloat. I thought about all of these things, and how, a week earlier, Jess told me, as she had requested, mother had a small service with only the family in attendance.

    We continued to wait, and people began to fidget and cough, and then we could hear cars pulling up outside. The governor and his wife came in, and then Laurel and her Aunt Janet appeared, both dressed in black and holding hands as they walked toward the front of the church. We stood up, and waited until they had reached their seats. Then, Reverend Stickles came out of a side door behind the altar. He was dressed in New Age velvet robes, covered with what seemed like hundreds of odd religious symbols. At the altar, Reverend Stickles stood with bowed head while Laurel and Janet sat down. Then, without looking up, he motioned for the congregation to be seated. I knew he loved dramatic pauses, and guessed we were in for one now. We waited until he slowly raised his head, leaned forward with an earnest expression, and launched out, "How many of you here today have ever noticed what happens when you put a teabag into a cup of water?" he whispered. I watched Jess, seated in front of me, as a tremor passed down his back, but this was probably because Laurel was there, and without warning I could feel a tremor that I didn't understand going down my own back.

    I knew that Leon was the dark stain that had poisoned all our lives, and I began to feel webs of relationships and motives developing, all wrapped around Leon sitting dead in his chair. I only had Jess left to talk to now, Jess, who sat frozen in his chair as Mama broke the plate over his head with one perfect blow, with the knife quivering in the wall behind me. And then there was Claire, waiting for me back in Boston. We met at a party in New Hampshire. She is a beautiful woman who is a reporter and always asks a lot of questions. I guess she must share the same DNA with Dr. Cranston, since both of them urged me to come back to North and deal with all of the issues in my life that I had tried not to think about.

I needed to call Claire and tell her about Leon's murder. I wasn't at all sure what I would tell Dr. Cranston when I got back to his office in Boston. So I decided to visit Jess and ask him what he thought about all of this, now that he was back home in North for good, and where he and Laurel, I was sure, were soon to be married.

TWO

"The Wedding-Guest Here Beat His Breast"

Women often complain that men become more attractive as they grow older, while women become less appealing, losing the fresh bloom of their beauty as they have children and gain weight. I don't believe this myself. Such complaints are just another sign of the usual preoccupation that some women like my ex-wife Marty have with their appearance, and perhaps, at a deeper level, they are part of the self-hatred all of us feel, which we express in different ways through the usual psychopathology of slips of the tongue, or jokes that are "unintentionally" directed back against ourselves.

I once told Dr. Cranston that people are always saying I look much younger than my age.

"Why does that bother you?" Dr. Cranston asked.

"It just reinforces my negative feelings about myself," I said, trying to sound cynically adult. "It makes me feel that people don't take me seriously."

Dr. Cranston just looked at me and said, "Maybe that's because you often present yourself in a very childlike way." I can still hear the hiss as the air escaped from my little balloon of assertion.

What can I say? We can never be really sure of the truth about other people's lives, not to mention the truth about our own little private hells. At least, that's what I believe. You can think what you want.

I came to New York after finishing college, on the run, you might say, after being told by Leon Putnam to leave Florida or else. My father had threatened to kill Leon after Leon's bank had taken over the acres of orange groves that surrounded our home. That was all, but it was enough. Leon didn't need to go into details, since earlier he had told Jess the same thing, when he found out that Jess was in love with his daughter Laurel.

Once settled, I began looking for work and trying to put Leon out of my mind by throwing myself into my new career and within a year by marrying a divorced woman named Marty Hanson, who had a nine-year-old daughter named Heather, who came to despise me. The marriage lasted three years, and as you are probably saying to yourself just now, what else could you expect.

I joined an up and coming new advertising firm in New York called Provenance, and became interested in market research early in my career. The firm took off as personal computer technology was implemented and information of all sorts became available on the Web. Suddenly, we were able to do a lot of things in-house that we had been outsourcing. I

took a chance, and started a market research group to supple-
ment the advertising and design work we were doing. It went
well. I became a Vice President three years after I joined the
firm, and the same month I divorced Marty, who had started
at Provenance a month before I signed on.

Marty always seemed unhappy, either with me or the
job or both, and our marriage seemed more and more like a
huge mistake. This could only last so long, however, and soon
after divorcing me, Marty resigned from the firm to start a
small magazine called IN LABOR, concerned, appropriately
enough, with women's issues. It got off the ground rather
quickly, but then plateaued out, and was about to go under
when it was bought by the Kawanaka media empire and ab-
sorbed into their list of faceless publications.

A year later, I received a wedding invitation from Marty, announcing her marriage to Spiros Kawanaka. There was a
personal note to me inside from both of them, saying that my
attendance would provide a wonderful sense of closure if I
came to their wedding. They were inviting all their "past families" to become part of the greater team of supporting loved
ones. A brochure designed by Marty was enclosed with the
invitation, with details about all the wonderful events planned
for our two-day visit. There were tellingly unflattering photographs of former spouses, myself included, together with
portraits of the coincidental in-laws, who were still "loved
very much." Last but not least, were snapshots of the children
from all their marriages past and up to and what almost the
present was; Spiros's last divorce having just become final a
few weeks before.

The good thing about market research is that it has
nothing to do with the everyday reality of North, the small
town in north Florida, and which I used to think was drably
predictable, until Leon's murder. At any rate, market research

helped me see that even in North there were layers of reality containing other worlds that exist next to the world I knew.

In market research, you can create places where you can go at any time if you have imagination, and the money to get there. Some of these places have familiar sounding names you might recognize, like the world of people over fifty who like to kayak or the world of single women over thirty-five with more than one cat. The trick is to create worlds that are interesting enough so that people want to go for a visit, and superficial enough so they will not stay long. Borrowing a neologism from our friends in beverage advertising, I think of these ideal worlds as lite worlds and our travel from one world to the other as travel in lite years. Once, for fun, I created something I called a "death app," which removed all the people who had died from your database.

I was sure that Marty's wedding existed in some unimaginable lite world designed for billionaire weddings, and that I would miss something important if I didn't make the trip. Of course, I wrote back immediately saying I would be there, and then called Jess, and told him about the wedding so he could say I told you so, since he had always said my marriage to Marty was doomed. Jess works in real estate, and lives near St. Simons Island, and the trip home to North takes him about two hours, which is close enough for an occasional visit with Laurel Putnam, Leon's daughter. Just before I hung up, Jess mentioned that I needed to be ready to come back home soon, since our mother's heart had started to fail from years of smoking and congestive heart failure. I never asked Jess about Laurel, since we knew that as long as Leon was alive, they would have to lead separate lives.

My story is complicated in a different way, since Marty had been married when we first met, and had a daughter, Heather, by the man Marty always referred to as "my first hus-

band." Heather was a precociously vicious child of ten, who
took me aside a few weeks before I married her mother, and
told me she thought I sucked. Then she told me why. What
impressed me most during this little session with Heather was
the specificity of the catalog she had evidently been keeping, which described in detail all my trespasses. It was a lovely summer afternoon at the beach house I had rented, and
Heather trapped me by leaning against the bedroom door, so
I couldn't escape, and then proceeded to hiss out my sins one
by one, delivering them with the regularity of hammer blows.
I couldn't wait to see her again.

Spiros Kawanaka, Marty's intended, was the product
of some weird coupling that could only happen in California.
His mother was the legendary Greek beauty Ismene Sarris,
who died while climbing Mount Olympus, disappearing into
the black clouds of a summer storm while striding upward
toward the gods. Her body, frozen in a fetal position, was
later recovered at the bottom of the mountain's famous south
gorge.

Spiros's father was the late Hitori (Jumbo) Kawanaka, so named for his ability to crush a competitor the way
an elephant crushes a peanut shell. Jumbo had built the first
modern media empire based on horizontal integration of the
new technology, and was famous for his terrifying *ahh . . .
huh!* sound, caused by a quick exhalation of breath, when, in
business meetings, he sensed an opponent had committed a
fatal error. He had six daughters by various wives, and was
almost an old man when his only son, Spiros, was born. Jumbo ran his companies with an iron hand, until he became too
senile to protect himself. Armed with a forged writ giving him
power of attorney, Spiros seized control one night in a coup,
carried out with the same timing for the fatal blow that had
made his father famous. It is rumored that when Spiros called

to give him the news, Jumbo, out cruising on his yacht, gave a final, quick ahh. . .huh! and fell to the deck clutching his chest.

The wedding was being held in San Francisco. Spiros had inherited five hotels, and he was simply taking over the most palatial hotel for the two days of wedding festivities. Travel directions by land, sea and air were included in Marty's brochure. There were also instructions on how to dress, and a two-day agenda for each carefully planned event. Finally, the loving couple requested that there be no wedding presents. Instead, Marty, in a canny moment of self-protective insight, had secretly negotiated with the Ugandan government for the creation of a new elephant preserve, to be named after Jumbo. Guests could, if they so desired, make donations. Spiros wept when, after the wedding, Marty announced how much money had been raised.

I was alone among the members of our little community at Provenance to be honored by a wedding invitation. The reaction at the firm when I announced that I would be away a few days to attend Marty's wedding was that strange mixture of relief and dread you see on the faces of those in the waiting room at the dentist's office; relief that someone else's name has been called instead of yours, and dread that even now, a chair intended for you is being vacated.

During her stay with us at Provenance, Marty wore extravagant clothes that were meant to impress, while at the same time, the eccentricity of her lack of style would show that underneath, she was, after all, a really important creative person. All of us try to do things like this, I suppose, but Marty had chosen capes and scarves and had never varied her routine. Final profound summations were her specialty, combined with a swirl of capes and scarves as she turned away, before you could say anything negative like, "That's the stupidest thing I've ever heard!"

The day I announced that I had made the A-list of wedding invitations, Marty called to check up on me. Had I received the invitation?

I quickly said yes, knowing what was coming.

As usual, she paused dramatically, and said, "Well, Hal, what do you think?"

Marty believed this was a clever ploy to make other people give their opinion first, but since she had been using this approach since I had known her, I was not unprepared.

I lobbed the ball back in her court, and said, "Well, Marty, I think it's the most incredible wedding invitation I've ever seen."

For some reason, Marty was always stumped by this kind of reply, and I could imagine her growing red in the face as she struggled to come up with a good continuing shot. I waited, knowing that since she would have to blurt out her news or die, time was on my side.

Finally, just before implosion, she gave in.

"Well . . . couldn't you find something nice to say, for God's sakes!"

There was another pause, and then, in a quieter tone, "Would you have ever thought I would end up marrying . . ."

There was a little sob, and her voice grew softer and then trailed off, but I knew what she wanted me to say, that wasn't it wonderful that after many ups and downs, little Marty Hanson was going to marry a billionaire who just happened to be the publisher of her failing magazine.

I amped up the sincerity in my voice.

"No Marty," I answered truthfully. "I wouldn't have thought it. Not in a million years," but then, trying not to sound too mean, I added, "But you've worked hard and you certainly deserve it."

There was a pause, and then Marty unexpectedly

moved off in another direction and asked "By the way, Hal, I was wondering if you remember the conversation we once had about a man named Leon Putnam?"

As it always did, the mention of Leon's name sent shivers up my back, and I gave a quick, involuntary gasp that I was sure Marty, ever alert, heard over the phone.

"Why are you asking me that?" I stammered, in a totally unconvincing voice, as I tried to deal with Marty's opening a door I thought I had closed forever, releasing a wave of dead, cold air that Leon's name and thoughts of my past always bring for me, thoughts of my childhood home in Florida, in North.

Ever alert, Marty realized that she had caught me off guard and didn't even bother to answer my question, saying only, "Tell me more about him. You remember, he bought your father's orange groves, or something like that."

I gave up any pretense of not knowing, and decided to concentrate on giving Marty only the minimal amount of information.

"He's been the Speaker of Florida's House of Representatives for most of my life," I said. "He's from the same small town in Florida I grew up in, a town called North."

"So you go way back?" Marty said.

I added, trying to sound non-committal, "We know some of the same people." We exchanged a few more volleys, and, after a pause, we said goodbye.

The lights in the city were twinkling on as I started packing for the trip west and the Kawanaka-Hanson nuptials.

It was raining when I left La Guardia on the nine a.m. flight for San Francisco, and it was raining when the plane landed that afternoon, after circling out over the Pacific for an extra half hour, just long enough to want an extra drink, but not long enough for the flight attendants to serve more than the lucky few in first class.

After the usual hassle with luggage and finding a cab, I thought about my last conversation with Marty, as I unpacked slowly in my hotel room, sipping on a cold gin and tonic and thinking over all the memories that had come surging back as Marty and I talked on the phone. I could make a decent guess about Leon and why Marty had asked about him. Spiros, the new husband, must be doing business big time somewhere in Florida, so naturally Leon's name had come up.

But I didn't want to think about North, that was years ago, and Leon had wrecked our lives so thoroughly that I had to leave for New York, departing in the middle of the night in an old, beat up Chevrolet.

My cell phone vibrated as I was unpacking. I picked it up, bracing myself for the irritating sound of Marty's voice, and trying to think of an excuse to get out of a dinner invitation, where, I was sure, Marty would want me to meet with some friends who would enjoy so much my showing them around San Francisco.

"Hello," I said, waiting for Marty to make the first move.

There was a long pause, and I heard a voice say, "Hello, Hal? This is Jess."

I wrote a note to Marty the next morning and left it at the desk; something about an illness, and needing to get home. The flight back to New York seemed to last forever, but I didn't care. Jess had told me that the doctors were talking about moving Mom to an ICU unit, and that I should think about leaving work on short notice. I started calling the few people at my office who would have to know about my change of plans.

I needed to finish some complicated changes in contracts a client had asked for, and the agreement over the details took longer than I expected, but thinking I had the time I stayed in New York to clear up the details. Three days later, as I was just signing the final papers, Jess called to say Mom had died and that I should stay and finish what I was working on. Mom had been unconscious most of the time since our last talk, and so I could finish up at work and come down for a visit and help with cleaning out the house we grew up in. Jess said that he would take care of the funeral expenses.

I wasn't sure what I would be facing in North so I stayed in New York two more days, telling people at the office I might be out on leave for two or three weeks. By the time I would reach North, my mother would have been dead for a week and Leon Putnam murdered as he sat in a chair at home, paralyzed and helpless.

THREE

Hal and Claire

It was early the next morning, after making frantic last-minute arrangements, that I found myself listening to the noises inside the cabin of the 747 as it headed south toward Jacksonville.

I tried to sort it all out, but my mind was still dazed by the cross country flight to California for my ex-wife's wedding, and then, because of Jess's call just after I had arrived at the motel in L.A., taking the next-day turnaround flight back to New York, then a week of frantic work, to the present, flying back south, as I sat listening to the muted roar of the jet engines and watched the flight attendants getting carts and trays ready, listening to the glasses clinking and wheels thumping as the carts rolled down the aisles, somehow these mingled noises reminded me of when, as a child, I pulled my heavy, homemade toy truck behind me. Bump, bump, bump.

As I listened to those imagined wooden crashes, and the sharp metallic sounds of the flight attendants pushing their carts, the absurdity of my accepting Marty's wedding invitation began to fade away, and the immediacy of where I was going, and having to face a trip back to North and the immediacy of Mom's death . . . all of this seemed unimaginable. All of these noises and conflicting thoughts and feelings suddenly existed inside me for a moment and then went silent, leaving me empty with no center, alone in this metal airborne capsule, surrounded by strangers, hurtling forward in space and time toward . . . what? The North I would soon be driving to from the airport would not be the North of my childhood, but a new North that I dreaded.

What would North be like with a paralyzed Leon Putnam, the black hole of the Sunshine State? Why had Marty asked about Leon? Was her husband worried about him? How would Jess and Laurel deal with Leon's death? And why in hell had I agreed to go to Marty's wedding in the first place?

As I flew south, I could look toward the eye of the storm brewing for me in Florida, knowing all that it meant, and feeling the ever-present sense of anxiety and despair that came in my dreams at night. I tried to put them out of my mind, but I couldn't, and instead, I entered the old nightmare about my mother's never even acknowledging my need to simply be loved, or at the very least, be approved of. In these dreams, as in my life, I was constantly standing in front of her asking for approval, which was never granted according to Dr. Cranston in my therapy sessions. He said she was psychotic.

I wanted to think about Claire, who was beautiful and fun loving and a reporter on a small Boston weekly that specialized in cultural events and the Boston social scene. She knew all the important people, the ones who are commonly referred to as "thought leaders in the field," as well as CEO's of major corporations and owners of art galleries. She always had invitations to the latest social occasions, and I enjoyed tagging along. We had gradually eased into an informal, almost serious relationship, with, as they say, benefits, and were reaching what you might call the major commitment phase, meaning that one of us would give up his or her apartment, and that we would start living together. I was trying to come to terms with this, and what it would mean.

Dr. Cranston, my therapist, had been encouraging full disclosure if I were really serious about Claire, and so I spent long nights talking with Claire about my family and where I grew up, and, of course, the people in North I grew up with, including Jess and Laurel and Leon Putnam, and how Leon had foreclosed on our orange groves, and about the night I saw him try to rape Nancy Ebersole. Through it all, Claire listened quietly, encouraging me to go on when I would say something like "Do you really want to hear all of this?"

It was calming to think about Claire as the jet reached altitude and leveled out. My mind floated back to a few weeks earlier, when her editor, Roger Bourne, had invited us for a weekend party at his family's summer home in New Hampshire.

Roger's two daughters, Linell and Kate, were in college, but had come for the weekend, and Roger and his wife Ann, the two daughters, and Claire and I made up the party for dinner. More guests were expected later for drinks.

We were all in high spirits, as who wouldn't be with a wonderful dinner of lobsters fresh off the boat, a fresh summer salad, corn on the cob and homemade potato chips. Linell and Kate filled our glasses with a cold, white wine, and we buttered our corn, and broke off a few lobster claws. I kept looking at Roger, but he was at the other end of the table, so I talked with Ann and Claire, who kept exchanging glances with Roger as we talked.

We finished eating, and before the other guests arrived, I saw Roger motion to Claire, and watched as they slipped quietly into his study, for what I assumed would be a talk about some assignment she was working on for the paper. It turned out to be more than that.

What I didn't know until our walk on the beach was that Claire had been telling Roger about our long talks at night, and filling him in on all the details about the people in North, and why I never went back to visit them, and how my mother's health was declining. Evidently, Roger seemed only mildly interested when she mentioned Leon Putnam. Claire said that Roger just waved his hand in a hurry up gesture as she told him what he evidently already knew, that Leon was one of the most powerful men in Florida, who, until his stroke, had served longer than anyone as the speaker of Florida's House of Representatives, but when she started adding the personal details I had told her about Leon's private life, including all that he had done to my family, and how, as a boy, I saw him try to rape Nancy Ebersole, his hand stopped waving and he leaned forward, eyes wide open.

It was then, I believe, after Claire had finished that Roger lowered the boom, telling Claire how all of the staff on the paper thought she could be a great reporter, but all she seemed interested in was the usual round of media interviews with the latest new person.

He told her that she was just coasting. "You can't even see the story that is right in front of you about this Leon Putnam."

Until then, Roger pointed out, it had never occurred

to Claire that she could use my stories as a beginning to write a profile for the paper.

"Keep talking to your friend, Hal," he advised. "Find out all you can and then go to Florida and talk to the people there, who they are and how they think about North and Leon Putnam. Did he have any friends? What is the town like? I don't want to hire somebody else to do the job you should be doing."

"Roger," Claire said, "meant this last sentence as an ultimatum."

While all of this was going on with Roger and Claire, I was busy helping Ann in the kitchen. After about ten minutes, the front doorbell rang, and Ann walked over to Roger's study and opened the door slightly, "Our guests are here."

Roger and Claire reappeared and I could hear Ann welcoming the other couples that had been invited for after dinner drinks, and the room was quickly filled with a surge of people I didn't know, and as we all said hello I moved to the kitchen and started helping Claire, who motioned for me to stay in the kitchen as she carried out the tray she had waiting. "I'll find out what they want to drink," she said. "Get out some glasses, and the liquor is in that cabinet."

I busied myself putting out glasses on the counter, and arranging some of the wine and liquor bottles.

After a moment, Claire came back with some orders. "Two gin and tonics, two white wines, one scotch and water, and a glass of milk."

"Milk!" I laughed.

"Somebody's pregnant."

I started making the drinks while Claire found a tray, and I glanced at her sideways as I carefully put the drinks down, counting each glass out loud. For a moment I thought she was crying—something she never did. She turned away and then gave me a quick look, and asked, "What's your therapist's name, again?"

"Arthur Cranston," I said, startled, "Why do you ask?"

There was a pause. I waited.

"I could be wrong," Claire said. "It's just that when you talk to me about your family and ex-wife, it seems to help you. Isn't that what Dr. Cranston says? Maybe you should talk more about this Putnam guy, and how he destroyed your family."

There was an edge in my voice that always comes out when somebody tells me I must do something, particularly something related to my family and the people in North.

"Why must I?"

"Because you don't want to know, and that's what always makes a good story, something is there you don't want to know, and can't say why."

"You aren't related to Dr. Cranston, are you?"

Claire laughed. "What does Dr. C. say?"

He says, 'There needs no ghost,'. . .

I stopped, and wonderfully, Claire finished with, 'come from the grave, my Lord, to tell us this.'

There was a click inside me, as if I knew that I had connected with someone I wanted to be with for more than just casual weekends, someone who was the opposite of Marty, and who could finish a line from Hamlet, and who, even if she didn't understand what was hidden in the past, wanted to know more about it. I suddenly knew that my relationship with Claire had moved closer to our being together for a long, long time. I hoped forever.

"I'm sure Dr. Cranston can quote from lots of things," Claire said. She picked up the tray of glasses and started to turn away.

"Take the drinks in, and let's go for a walk on the

beach," I said. "Tell Ann we won't be long."

Claire looked at me and then walked through the door and into the wall of laughter and talk coming from the living room.

Little Boar's Head sits at the far end of Hampton Beach, which curves south for about three miles to Big Boar's Head, where the road narrows and continues south before ending at a state park. A radar site used to sit on top of Big Boar's Head, but was demolished years ago. There was a moon, and so we didn't need a flashlight as we walked past the lawns of darkened houses toward the road that crossed Little Boar's Head and then dropped steeply down to the beach. We crossed the road and slid down a sandy hill, sand dunes really, winding through them to the more level ground near the darker line where the tide was coming in, and then, the idea hitting us both at the same time, we took our shoes off and piled them up together to mark the path to the road. The wind blew the salt air into our faces and we began to walk toward the distant lights of Hampton Beach.

"What happened in Florida that you don't want to find out? I need to know so Roger won't fire me. It sounds crazy but it's true. He said I had to learn to recognize a story, since they are almost always buried under things that are unimportant. Finding out more about Leon Putnam is a test to see if I can do that."

"Too much happened to tell during a walk on the beach," I said. Then, trying to give her a chance to say why she had been crying, I added, "Why, is there something you don't want to talk about?"

"No, my problem is just the opposite. I tell everything. In my family, nothing was hidden. We could talk about anything, but the talking didn't do much good."

"I thought talking was the medicine that cured all ills."

"My father was an alcoholic. Everybody knew it so there was nothing to hide. We could talk about it all we wanted, since everybody else did. The year after he died, I went away to college, and then married the wrong man. The divorce was final last year. You and I celebrated it in a very nice way, if you remember."

She went on. She was right. She was a talker.

"I think the world is divided into two kinds of persons, those who have been damaged and know what has happened to them, and those who were damaged but don't know. I'm the first kind, the kind who knows."

"And I'm the second kind?"

"I'm just guessing, but let's say that for now the answer is yes, that you were damaged and don't know."

"And knowing it would help me in some way?"

Claire paused for a moment, and gave a tight, bitter smile. "When my dad came home drunk and slammed me and my brother across the room, and did even worse things to my mom, it wasn't hidden. There was no pretense or sugar coating. I can look back now and say that's what happened to me. That's what made me the way I am."

Thinking that I could see where she was going, I said, "My dad wasn't a drinker."

Claire laughed, and said, "And you're not either, and believe me, I know one when I see one. I'm just saying that I know that talking about things doesn't mean you won't have problems, but that you can't really start to help yourself until you understand your own history, and how to see the world from someone else's point of view. Look at me. Tonight Roger just told me that I had to learn how to recognize a story, and that if I didn't, I would soon be out of a job. He meant learn about Leon Putnam and all that—the stuff you know more about than you know the hidden things about your own life.

At the risk of sounding sickeningly sincere, I said, "So what do you think is wrong with me?"

Claire didn't even pause. "I think that whenever you start to say something about yourself, you already feel sure that it won't interest anyone."

"How do you know I feel that way?"

"I can see it in your eyes. When you talk about North and Leon Putnam and your family in Florida, this vacant look comes over your face, as if you suddenly had no idea what to say."

We walked on toward the lights and I tried to understand what was going on. I knew that Claire was probably right, and that I felt an almost unacknowledged fear because she was so intent on getting me to talk about my past, and what it meant to me, and why she felt so strongly that I should go back home to North. I wouldn't learn until later that she intentionally left out that Roger not only wanted her to find out more about Leon, but that he had ordered her to follow me, and start looking for a story.

As we walked, I could feel things surging up in me that I didn't want to think about, and, as always, I pushed these thoughts away, so I stopped and said, "Let's go back."

We turned around, and then, with no warning Claire hoisted up her skirt and said, "Race you to our shoes!" and began running with a beautiful gliding motion toward the dark mass of Little Boar's Head. I went sprinting after her, but couldn't catch up. She was a wonderful runner, hardly seeming to touch the sand as her bare feet noiselessly left her footprints in front of me and her legs flashed in the moonlight in a silver blur.

She waited for me, laughing as I came galumphing up. She looked incredibly desirable, and I reached out and put my arm around her. "If I go to Florida, I won't be here to tell you about my mysterious past," I said, pulling her toward me. We kissed, and then put on our shoes and walked back through the dunes to the road. When we got to the steep bank, I went first, and put out my hand to her at the top and didn't let go as we walked back together in the moonlight. The next morning, we had a breakfast of hot coffee and sweet rolls, and said our goodbyes to Ann and Roger.

Back in Claire's apartment we unpacked and, late that night, we began talking about the party. Claire was amazed when I casually mentioned that I liked the old Morris chair sitting in the corner of the Bourne's living room, and then went on to describe the room in detail.

"How do you do that?"

I told her about my finger method, and how, whenever I go on a visit to some place I've never been before, I try and memorize the layout of the rooms. It's simple to do. For example, say it's this weekend, at Roger Bourne's, and we're sitting in the living room talking, and I start with my left thumb. That's number one, and, in my mind, I place number one over the large red sofa with the rattan back that sat up against the front wall. Then, number two, my left index finger, went over the large cast iron stove made by the Vermont Castings Company at the far end of the room. I go around the room like this, assigning a number and a finger to the major items in the room and trying to keep the number of items identified to ten or under.

When I finish, there is a long pause.

"Do you do this a lot?" Claire asks in a quiet, nervous way.

"All the time."

"But why?"

"I don't know. It's just a way of remembering things. The Morris chair becomes connected to everything else that happened at the party, and it all comes back to me in a way that somehow seems not just real, but more than real."

Claire's eyes widened. "That's what I need to do. When I write a piece for the paper, it has to be accurate and true, that is not made up. But to keep the reader interested, I need to make a story for the paper seem . . . not just real, and not made up like fiction . . . I need to make it seem more than real, with details like the Morris chair and the cast iron stove.

The next morning, I saw Claire off for work, and then caught the shuttle back to New York, promising her all the while that things would work out.

FOUR

The Photograph

There is a dead tree that has come down outside the window of my father's old study. I can see the stump sticking out of the small bushes that mark the border between the grass and the woods beyond the house. My mother's latest found dog, Mac, is digging frantically around the stump, following the scent of a mole. Watching him reminds me of the many dogs we had when I was growing up, all of them "found" as my mother liked to call them, though only Pickle, a pup shivering by the side of the road, was really found. The others, June, Ham, Syd, and Maisie came from the local animal shelter, where mother rescued them from the grim door of the large incinerator where the dogs whose time had run out ended up.

I am not sure what will happen to Mac, now that my mother is dead. My brother Jess doesn't want him, though Jess would be the logical choice since he lives in North now, with Laurel. Thinking back through the long list of the dogs mother kept when I was growing up, I can only remember the names of the last few, since many of them are only dim memories floating out there in the dream-like time of early childhood. Jess, since he is older, can remember the names of others. His favorite was a golden cocker spaniel named Taffy. It seems strange to imagine Jess, like mother's dogs, existing before me.

Many of these dogs met untimely ends, as mother would say. Maisie got too close to a tractor in our orange grove, and Syd fell asleep on the road one night, and was run over by a car, and since he was black, the driver never even saw him, or so he said. Mother's reaction was to shrug and say how she tried to warn Syd about the road. She would wait a few weeks, and then she would get another dog. "Syd had a good life," she said, "and it was his time to go."

I guess you could say that about all of us, although when I said that about Leon's death, Laurel thought I was being cruel. Maybe so. I didn't mean it that way. It was a phrase I remember mother saying, and it just popped out, so to speak. I often say things like that, and don't understand what I have really said until someone like Laurel points it out. I realize there is a deep truth in cruelty, but people don't always want to hear it, and besides, the truth may be more about my state of mind than anything else. Anyway, I know Jess felt the same way I did about Leon, even if he didn't let on.

I could use some backup now, given what I have found in our house. It seemed the logical thing to Jess and me when we met after mother's funeral, and we both agreed that I should be the one to go through the rooms of our house, with all their closets and drawers, and decide on what stays, what goes to Goodwill and what we will throw away. Jess and Laurel were busy with their own house, doing lots of renovations in a place that had not been lived in for years, and so I had agreed to make a start, though I made Jess promise that he would come over to see what I was keeping and what I was throwing away.

I had started in a room that was originally my father's study, and then it became a storage room and a sewing room. There was a heavy oak desk against the wall, and the last drawer I opened had an old cigar box inside, with sewing pins, buttons and thread. I picked it up to examine it, and decided to throw it away, when I saw a stack of photographs underneath the box. Most of them were faded, and had been taken with old cameras that have almost disappeared, but one of the pictures, carefully placed on the bottom of the stack, was in full color, and seemed new, not taken by my mother, I thought, who never took pictures of anything. The picture was taken in a public park in Palatka, and showed a small crowd gathered around a platform where people were giving someone an award.

Whoever took the picture either had no talent for it, or was focusing on something else, because the platform and the award ceremony were off to the side of the picture and hard to see. Almost all of the people in the small crowd, however, were clearly identifiable. I held the picture up to the window for more light, and after a moment, I could see that the person getting the award was (who else?) Leon Putnam. Probably Leon had secured a small grant to improve the park, which I remembered from my childhood, and was being recognized for it. I don't really know, and probably never will.

I wondered why on earth my mother would save this picture of a man who had destroyed our lives. I began examining the photograph more carefully, looking for clues. I will always regret doing this, since, almost immediately, I could see someone I knew, standing at the far edge of the crowd. It was Sarah Ebersole, Nancy's mother. I stood in the light from the window and studied the photograph carefully, and I could tell that Sarah was not looking up at the platform, as you would expect, but seemed to be looking at someone else across the semi-circle of the crowd around the platform. I took my finger, and traced a line across the photograph, following the direction of her glance.

At first, I couldn't see anything familiar, because the people near the edge of the crowd, on the side from which the picture was taken, had their backs turned away from the camera, and were watching the platform. I studied the photograph again, tracing the line of Sarah's gaze across the crowd, with my finger always stopping at the same place, where a woman was standing, her face slightly turned away from the platform, so I could see a glimpse of her profile, looking directly, it seemed, back at Sarah, on the other side of the crowd. Probably I will never know for certain, but I am almost sure, now, that this other woman, the one looking back at Sarah, was my mother.

I was about to put the photograph back on top of the desk when I happened to look on the back. I could see some writing in faded ink and looking more closely I could identify my mother's writing. Something about "in the hands of the law now" or "in the land of the law now" or something like that. What followed was, to me, nothing more than two lines of a series of meaningless numbers and letters. This had obviously meant something to my mother but the key to what she meant to preserve was now lost with her.

I turned to put it back on the desk when Mac's barking brought me out of the trance, and I looked to see Jess standing in the doorway, looking at me in that amused way he has as his eyes glanced around the room. "Did you find something interesting?" he asked. I didn't reply but walked over and handed him the photograph.

"See anybody you know?" I said. Jess held up the photograph and squinted. "Go over to the window, the light is better there, and you'll need it."

Jess walked over to the window and held up the photograph to the light. After a moment he said, "Damn! That's Leon Putnam."

I knew it wouldn't take Jess long to find Leon up on the platform, where most people would look first, and I waited for a second and then said, "Keep looking."

Jess gave me a frown, and held the photograph up again. After a moment he shrugged. "I don't recognize anyone else up on the platform."

"Look in the crowd," I said. "Start with the far side, the side with the people facing you, and look toward the end."

Jess looked puzzled and held up the photograph again. I waited. After a moment his back jerked and he leaned closer toward the photograph. "Isn't that... Sarah Ebersole, Nancy's mother?"

"That's what I think." Jess gave me a hard look, and said, "So what if it is?"

"There's something else," I said. "Don't you think she's looking at someone on the other side of the crowd? Follow the direction of her gaze."

Jess looked for a long time, and then said, "You can't really tell anything. The people on that side are turned away from you."

I walked over and put my finger on Sarah, then traced the line of her gaze across the crowd, to the other woman on the near side, with her face turned slightly, as if looking back at Sarah. "See that woman?" I said. "That's our mother."

Jess gave me an incredulous look, and then turned back to the photograph. After a moment, he shook his head and said "No, sorry, Hal, she could be anybody. You're really reaching."

"What about the dress," I said. "I remember that dress. And that's the way she always wore her hair. Look at the profile. You know I'm right."

Jess looked again, and then nodded a slow, reluctant nod almost agreeing. "I'll admit, it could be her. But you'll never prove it in court. And, again, so what if it is her? Tell me what it means."

I looked hard at Jess. "That's what we need to talk about." Jess looked back at me, "Start talking."

I started with the easy stuff for me, but harder for Jess. "What about Laurel? Has she ever talked about Mom and her dad?"

Jess looked away for a moment. "Well, she has talked about our losing the orange groves. She knows Leon was involved in some way. What are you driving at?"

"Has she ever mentioned any kind of…" I paused, searching for the right way to put it. "Any kind of personal relationship kind of stuff."

Jess flushed, and said "You've got to be kidding. You mean Mom and Leon? That's way out of bounds." Jess looked away. "If there was something going on, it would be her wanting to kill Leon, if you want to call that a relationship."

Jess's using the word "kill" gave everything away. It was in his mind, too, but he just wasn't conscious of it, yet. I pushed harder. "What if it wasn't so simple. Not just a man wanting a woman, but something more complicated."

"Like what?" Jess shot back.

"Like blackmail," I said. "What if it was some kind of

blackmail."

I was guessing here. I was almost certain that Jess knew nothing about that day long ago when Mama and Sarah Ebersole, Nancy's mother, had made me testify about what I saw Leon do to Nancy that evening at the graduation party, pinning her against the dock and pulling her bathing suit off.

Jess considered my blackmail statement for a moment. "I don't think so. What would she have on Leon that she could threaten him with? Besides, Leon always covered his tracks. He couldn't have survived that long otherwise."

Jess's response told me he didn't know about Leon assaulting Nancy. I paused, and went on without saying anything about what I knew.

"Mom and Nancy Ebersole weren't in Palatka to hear about what a great man Leon Putnam was. They were there for a reason."

Jess put the photograph down and walked toward the door. "Maybe so, but I don't think we will ever know what the reason might be."

Jess walked out into the hallway, then stopped and looked back at me. "Let me know when you're ready to call Mutt Cox. He can have someone haul all of this away."

The sound of Jess's steps grew fainter and fainter. I looked around and decided to call it a day, and began cleaning up. Before leaving, I picked up the photograph to take back to my room for another look. After supper, I began examining the photograph in detail, tracing each figure with my finger and pausing to look at each one. The last person on the platform where Leon was standing was a big state trooper, off to one side. My finger paused on him, and started to tremble as I recognized who he was. He was the trooper standing on the porch at Leon's house, that day on the dock when I was watching the divers search the lake for evidence.

FIVE

The State Trooper

Reporters are supposed to be good at asking questions. At least that is what most people seem to think. They are driven to know something, to look for reasons why something happened. And of course, the big question for me back home in North is finding out who killed Leon. As the song goes, 'If they asked me, I could write a book,' but most of what I could write now would just be conjecture. My solution is to start with a question that, I thought, might have a much smaller answer than the one about Leon. That is, who was the policeman standing on the dock that day watching the divers, and why was he also in the photograph my mother had, almost hidden in the desk drawer of my dad's old office desk?

I've been giving this policeman a lot of thought because I remember noticing him standing on the porch as I left Leon's house. At the time, I remember thinking that he looked quiet and withdrawn, and it seemed that he wasn't there just to protect a crime scene. But as I moved past him and felt these things, I put them out of my mind as I walked toward my car.

Now he was back in my mind again because in the photograph of Leon in Palatka, there he was, standing on the platform, and still looking quiet and withdrawn. Of course, I already had some possible answers that might fit him. Probably, he was Leon's bodyguard, on assignment from the State Police. Had someone threatened Leon? Maybe, but surely there would be more than one policeman on duty for a threat to the House Speaker, and if he had been assigned to protect Leon, where was he when Leon was killed?

And another question needs to be answered: When was the photograph taken? I thought Laurel might know something about the event in Palatka, and, even closer to home, she might know if the same policeman was on duty when Leon was killed.

Two nights later, I was sitting with Jess and Laurel at the supper table. They had asked me over to discuss things, and we had talked about Leon's funeral, who was there and who wasn't, and the long list of people Laurel had to sort out from the guest book where they had signed their names. We were in Leon's house, the house Laurel grew up in, not the one she and Jess had started fixing up for themselves, and they now had to decide on whether to change plans and move in to Leon's big house on the lake where we were now having supper, or go for the house they were fixing up, or just sell everything in North and go somewhere that would be free from all the memories they both had of North and their former lives. They both seemed happy and exhausted. Laurel was anxious, knowing, as she put it, that it would take her a long time to put Leon's affairs in order. There would be a reading of the will and probably a lot of discoveries about things that Leon had done that she didn't even want to know about. Lawyers would be waiting, she was sure.

As a change of pace, I pulled out the photograph of the ceremony at the park in Palatka and handed it to Laurel, and asked if she knew when it had been taken. She recognized the park, but after looking at it briefly she said that she remembered Leon getting some kind of award, but she hadn't been there, and she didn't know much about it. Leon had to attend multiple functions like that almost every week and she hadn't gone to many of them.

"What's important about it?" she wanted to know.

"It was in a drawer in my dad's old workroom, the one Mama used as sort of a storeroom."

Laurel looked at it again. "Dad looks older, like he did these last few years, so it could be fairly recent. Why did your mother save it?"

"I'm not sure," I said, trying to read her reaction, "except that she and Sarah Ebersole were there together in the crowd.

Laurel looked surprised, and nothing more, with no hint of something being uncovered that she might be worried about. She held the photograph up to the light and looked again. After a moment, her face brightened.

"Oh, yes, I can see her now. That is Mrs. Ebersole. But I don't see your mother."

I stood up and reached across the table and put the photograph on the table in front of her, and then put my finger on what we could see of Sarah Ebersole standing in the crowd.

"Do you see how her face is turned as if she's looking at somebody?"

Laurel nodded, "Okay, but what is she looking at?"

I put my finger on Sarah and moved it across the photograph in the direction of Sarah's gaze and stopped. "See that person? That's my mother."

"Our mother," Jess corrected, "if that's who it really is."

Laurel glanced at Jess. "You're not sure?"

"It could be her," Jess said, but I'm not as certain about it as Hal is."

"And something else," I said. "Look how her head is turned, as if she were looking back at Mrs. Ebersole."

"Well, maybe," Laurel said. "But Jess is right. You can't really say for sure." She shrugged and laughed. "See anybody else you know?"

I could tell she wasn't expecting me to say it, so when I said yes, she looked startled.

"See the state trooper on the platform? I know him."

Laurel looked at the photograph and laughed.

"Well, so do I. He was almost always assigned to Dad's security group. So what?"

"I was standing on the dock with Sheriff Moses the day he and the divers were here, a couple of hours before the funeral was to start. The trooper in the photograph was standing behind us on the porch."

"The governor or somebody probably wanted security here, as a favor to me," Laurel said. "And I think I did ask about it when I talked to his secretary. Why is it so important?"

"I don't know. I was here that day looking for you, and I walked past him on my way back to the car. It was strange. He didn't look like he was there for security reasons. He didn't even ask me who I was. It was like he didn't want to be noticed. I don't think the sheriff even saw him."

There was a pause. I could tell Jess and Laurel were ready to drop the subject. I gave it one more quick shot.

"You wouldn't know his name, would you?"

Laurel smiled, "Oh, sure. It's Douglas . . . Douglas Brunson."

I spent the next day revisiting the past by cleaning out all of the useless things all families accumulate over a long lifetime in a house, though nothing turned up that would help me answer some of the questions raised by the photograph of the crowd at the ceremony in Palatka. It seemed like everything circled back to Mama and Sarah Ebersole and why they were there together. I knew it couldn't be random. They both wouldn't just show up in the crowd at the same time by accident. And since Mama was dead, there was no one else to ask but Sarah Ebersole. What made it so intriguing was that they were the ones who tightened the screws on Leon years ago, after I saw Leon try to rape Nancy at Laurel's graduation party.

Of course, last night at supper, I couldn't mention that to Laurel, since I was sure she didn't know about it. So, late in the afternoon, I found myself driving up to Sarah's front yard and parking in the driveway, wondering what, exactly, I was going to say.

The Ebersoles lived on one of many small lakes in the area. It seems that when I was growing up, everybody I knew lived on a lake. Sarah and Mac, her husband, lived in an old country home with a large screened-in back porch that looked out on a lake with water so pure that a pipe ran from the house to the lake for drinking water.

I couldn't remember the last time I had seen her. She wasn't at Leon's funeral, for reasons I understood, and Jess said she wasn't at Mama's funeral either. I guessed that was because of her grief over Nancy's death. Sarah and Nancy had been close, and now Sarah was at home alone, with both her husband and her youngest daughter dead. Probably, she wasn't ready for the crowds at a funeral.

I knocked at the door and Sarah opened it, and I found myself looking at someone I almost didn't recognize. Her hair was gray, long and stringy and unkempt. She had on a shapeless dress and her shoulders were stooped. Her arthritic hands were gnarled and clutching the door for support. My face must have shown the shock and sadness I felt looking at her, and in a low, almost inaudible voice she said, "Hello, Hal. I thought you might be coming by."

She stepped back and motioned me in with her hands, as she shuffled off in front of me. I closed the door and followed her into the kitchen where she stopped at the big wooden table that I remembered from the few childhood visits I had made here, with Mama towing me along with the promise that we wouldn't stay but just a few minutes. There was a pot of coffee on the stove, and I remembered that, too. Mama always said that Sarah would have the coffee ready. Sarah sat down and looked at me.

"My hands aren't too steady. Pour us some coffee and have a seat." I looked around and she said, "The cups are in the cabinet over the stove. The sugar is on the table and there is a small pitcher of milk in the refrigerator, if you need it."

I thanked her and found two cups, poured the coffee and sat down, feeling the ghost of Sarah's old hospitality fill the room. When I looked at her, she ducked her head and smiled at me, the way she used to when I was a little boy, and I could see that behind the physical mask of old age, Sarah's inner self, the one I remembered, was still there, alert to the moment we were in now, and willing herself to be there.

Not sure of how to begin, I started with the usual words that seemed so insufficient, and yet necessary—saying how sorry I was about Nancy, and how I had not heard about her death until a few weeks after she died. Sarah said nothing and let me talk. Then she leaned forward and, looking at me intently all the while, she said that she understood, and that we needed to talk about something else. I waited, sensing that I didn't need to say anything.

"Well, well," she said as a little preamble. Then she pointed her index finger at the table and tapped it for emphasis. "Mac is dead, and now, so is Nancy, and, I guess, I won't be long behind them." She paused, and took a quick breath. "Did you know that Nancy died happy?"

Since I no longer lived in North, and hadn't seen Nancy for years, I didn't know what Sarah was trying to say. "I know that must mean a lot to you," I finally managed.

We looked at each other for a moment, as the long whine of an outboard motor moved past on the lake behind Sarah's house. I hadn't heard the sound of an outboard motor in a long time. Growing up, I knew boats going by on the lake behind our house, and Jess and I could identify the owner by the sound of the engine. Sarah noticed my look and said, "That's Harvey Wilson, checking on his bait lines."

"I never met Nancy's husband," I said. "I'm glad they were happy."

"Her husband," Sarah almost hissed. "His name is Michael, and he didn't make her happy. No, he did not. He lied to her. He said he loved her and then had an affair with Laurel Putnam."

I tried to take it in, but I was still dazed by the idea of Laurel, who loved Jess and was finally with him as she should have been all her life, having an affair with Nancy Ebersole's husband. Sarah gave a slight smile, as if she had finally been able to tell someone who needed telling the news she had been holding back.

"I said that Nancy died happy, and she did, but it wasn't because of Michael, her husband. No, she finally met a good man that loved her, and at least for a few months she was happy . . ." Sarah paused trying to say the words, "before she died."

All I could think about was Jess, and what, if anything, Laurel had told him about her affair with Nancy's husband. The long whine of Harvey Wilson's outboard grew louder again as he came back, heading in the opposite direction. I tried to focus on what Sarah had said. "What else did Nancy tell you?" I asked, thinking it was better to be direct.

"Nancy wanted to die at home," Sarah said. "She always felt ashamed about what happened that night at the lake with Leon, and with all of her friends at the party nearby, if not looking on. Especially since it was Laurel's party, and Laurel's daddy right there, then almost trying to rape Nancy at the dock."

"But nobody saw it but me, and I never said anything, except to Mama."

"I know, Hal. You did the right thing, but sometimes the right thing turns out to be wrong. Nancy always felt that nobody stood up for her and took her side, and so she ended up feeling that what happened was her fault. Your mother and I confronted Leon, and he agreed to help Nancy with a monthly payout, but it all had to be done in secret. We were afraid to go against Leon in public, and that's what was missing. Nancy needed that verdict, not in court, but an acknowledgement out in the open, and maybe that's why she never got over it. I don't know, it might have helped Nancy feel better about herself, but by then the damage had been done, and it was probably too late. Some things you can't undo."

"And her marriage to . . ."

"Michael," Sarah said.

"That didn't help?"

Sarah shook her head. "No, Michael made it worse."

"Did you ever meet the man she did fall in love with?"

"Not until after Nancy died. But Nancy told me all about him when she came home, that last time. It was so good to see her happy. Even though she was dying, she seemed contented, somehow. He came by to see me later, after she was gone, and I could tell that he really loved her."

"What was he like?" I said, sensing that she wanted to keep talking.

"He was a big man," she said. "A loner, I think. He ran away from home early, according to Nancy, and had lived all over the world. He was in the army, and then went into police work."

I kept up my questions. "How did they meet?"

Sarah gave me that smile again. "Leon sent him to check up on her."

"What!"

"Oh yes," Sarah said. "Leon had lots of people that he kept tabs on. After all, some folks might say we were black-mailing him. Leon needed any kind of information that he could use against people if he ever had to."

"Information about Nancy?" I said, not believing that even Leon would do this.

"That's right. The policeman said that the first time he met Nancy, he just knocked on her door and asked if she had seen any strangers in the neighborhood, and she invited him in. That's how it started, but then they fell in love, which was something Leon hadn't counted on."

I could hear myself giving a strange kind of laugh. "And you say he was a policeman!"

"That's right," Sarah said. "One of those state troopers. But he turned out to be a good man who loved Nancy."

"What was his name?" I asked, not seeing for a minute the answer that was coming.

"It was Douglas," Sarah said. "Douglas Brunson."

I sat back against the chair breathing hard.

"Are you all right," Sarah asked.

"I'm fine."

"Have some more coffee. That will settle you down."

"Damn!" I said, feeling a surge of anger, as if I were dealing with people who were holding out on me, and who, at the same time, didn't really know what they were doing. I reached for the photograph of the ceremony in Palatka and showed it to Sarah. "Do you remember this? You, Mama, Leon and Douglas Brunson are all in it."

Sarah looked at it for a moment, and her face grew hard and angry. "It's time for you to go," she said, and stood up.

SIX

Laurel and Michael

T he hour ended, and at various doors adjacent to the lawn writhing knots of students suddenly appeared, emerging in slow extrusions like newborn insects, before moving off in wavering files, as if still unsure where the scented air would lead them. Many of the students had book bags strapped to their backs, and almost all of them were thinking that next week, finally and for real, they would, at last start reading some of the books they had carried all semester, a necessary task, a few of them vaguely suspected, if they wanted to pass their final examinations.

It was ten in the morning. At the edge of the grass near the administration building, a sprinkler twirled lazily, forming a liquid rose that shivered whenever the transparent wind brushed past. The lawn, as always, was almost perfect, but not quite, the despair of the grounds crews, who struggled to eliminate the occasional sandy spots that migrated across the grass like a virulent attack of dandruff.

Some of the students strolled lazily by, while others, hurrying to make a class, loped along in diffident strides, barely able to conceal their sense of urgency. Spring term was almost over. Untroubled by the brightness of the morning, and spotted by bird droppings, marbled Homer stood unblinking in front of Davis Hall, gripping his harp, stone blind in amazement at what continually passed in front of him.

From where she stood on one of the walks that crossed the lawn, Laurel Putnam, a neatly attractive woman of thirty-two, watched the students moving in their thousand opposing ways, which somehow produced an overall impression of uniformity, like that of a moving battalion of ants. Only the years change, Laurel thought. The students are always the same; the same age, the same problems, and the same hopes that will soon be betrayed, if they haven't been betrayed already. Laurel sympathized with Homer, cemented to his pedestal, and forced to participate in the same processions that bound her own life, through all the cycles of time and weather.

Turning down an alley that cut behind the West Range, Laurel emerged on the sidewalk, crossed the street and began walking toward the library. Three floors above the crowded walkways, James Harrison, one of the graduate students who worked in Laurel's department, was standing on the flat part of the library roof near the front of the building. A door was open behind him, embedded in the roof where it slanted upward toward a golden weather vane. Laurel knew that the door opened on a stairway that went down into the attic, a large, dusty cavern that hung above the top floor of the library like a hive. Laurel also knew that Harrison could not see her as she walked under the trees toward the imposing stone steps that led up to the library doors.

Harrison sidled over to the wrought iron railing that edged the roof and leaned over. He pulled out what must have been a small coin from his pocket and tossed it toward a group of students standing on the steps below. Laurel could see the glint of metal as the coin dropped earthward, only to hit a tall, red-haired boy on the head and bounce in the air, still sending out bursts of reflected light as it spun in a high arc through the morning brightness. The red-haired boy gave a cry and involuntarily looked up toward the roof, but Harrison had ducked back through the door and was now out of sight. The coin hit the steps with a metallic click. Laurel continued upward toward the group of boys. She bent down and secured the coin, a new nickel, showed the coin to the tall boy who stood rubbing his head.

"Heads for luck," she said, pocketing the coin, as she continued on up the steps. She walked through the imposing doors, bypassed the security screen, and cut across the lobby, disappearing down a flight of steps that led to the Rare Books Division, where she was Assistant Director.

Harrison, just coming down from the attic, was innocently taking a seat behind the front desk, next to a flashy blond girl, the student assistant on duty until noon. Laurel could never remember the girl's name. Harrison leaned toward her as if to start a conversation. Laurel took out the coin, walked up to the desk and placed it in front of Harrison, with Jefferson's face turned down on the green mat of the desk.

"Tails, you lose," she said. Harrison looked down at the coin and his mouth gaped open. The blond assistant gave an uneasy laugh, not really sure what Laurel intended. "I sent you up to the attic to unload boxes. I can't have you throwing things off the roof," Laurel said evenly. Harrison looked up at Laurel, who looked down at Harrison with an expressionless stare. Realizing that something unpleasant was about to happen, the blond girl seemed to shrink, then hurriedly turned away, her face a mask of objective disinterest.

"I don't think it's a good idea for you to keep coming here," Laurel said. "You can leave now." Laurel nodded toward the door and smiled a bright, knowing smile of triumph at Harrison, then walked away. She knew that Harrison was a friend of someone important on the Board, and that more than likely she couldn't get his dismissal to stick. But that was all right. Probably, he would be so embarrassed that he wouldn't want to come back, even if the Head Librarian caved in and allowed it, which, Laurel was sure, he would.

Laurel also knew that she could have simply called her father, Leon Putnam, and explained the situation, and board member objections or no, Harrison would not return to the library. But she had learned long ago to never use her father's name as a threat, since, within Florida's borders, at least, he was without opposition. Laurel also knew that others might point out that she owed her job at the university library to her father's influence, but that didn't trouble her. She was good at her work, and her appointment had not hurt anyone—an unusual consequence of her father's influence.

Still, she thought, sitting down at her desk, it was satisfying to nail Harrison, to whom she had taken an instant dislike when they first met. Too bad she couldn't include the silly blond as part of the package.

Laurel settled in for the day's work. Over the past three years, in a desultory way, she and her staff had been unpacking the Steadman Collection, a miscellaneous pile of World War Two memorabilia put together by an almost forgotten graduate of the university, the egomaniacal Ralph Steadman, a junior Under Secretary of State at the end of the war, who had evidently been flown all over the world at the taxpayer expense so he could pick up or steal anything that was, in any way, attached to him by the nature of his office. Certainly, Laurel thought, looking at the catalog of items she was putting together, there was nothing that indicated a public mind capable of judicious statecraft or bold leadership, nothing that even hinted at a capacity for insight into the postwar political order, however unimaginative the insight might be.

It was also telling, she thought, that out of all the materials in Steadman's collection, there was never a move toward introspection, no journal with impressions of great and near great statesmen encountered, no letters with descriptive raptures over Venice or Paris, not even a slightly veiled love affair or two. And not surprisingly, Laurel thought, absolutely no mention of his family; a wife (long suffering, Laurel was sure, and now resting next to the redoubtable Ralph) and a son who still lived nearby.

Instead, the items cataloged so far included such gems of historical importance as a sign with Steadman's name on it, and placed in front of his limousine at an official state dinner; ashtrays, napkins, and menus from an endless procession of expensive restaurants in cities where he had dined with undersecretaries from other countries; tickets from airplanes, trains, and ocean liners; stacks of programs from theaters and concert halls where Steadman had sat dumbly in attendance; countless small clippings from the back pages of newspapers in various world capitals announcing his arrivals and departures, with the name *Steadman* carefully underlined in black ink; and, finally, a really decent collection of World War Two posters from around the world. These posters had been packed away in boxes, and were part of the stash being unloaded by the unfortunate Harrison, who, Laurel hoped, was now slinking toward his room and cursing her name.

From a professional standpoint Laurel acknowledged the value of the posters, but personally she had no interest in such material. War was just another chance for men to strut around like boys and act important. All of the items on her list, in fact, reminded her of nothing more than a boy's collection of baseball cards, only all of these cards had Steadman's name on them. And who, Laurel thought, would care about Steadman in another hundred years.

There was a hurried knock at the door. Michael Tuttle came in, looking cool and elegant as usual. He was a thin man with a narrow, black mustache, and was constantly cleaning his glasses with a pocket-handkerchief, which he kept in his hand and waved around like an actor in a Restoration comedy. Michael, who had been her lover for the past year and a half, was married to Nancy, one of the Ebersoles, who had, in fact, grown up in North and was the girl who had been attacked by Leon the night of the graduation party. Laurel knew nothing of this because Nancy told only her mother what Hal had seen as he swam near the dock that night. Not knowing this history, Laurel called her "the fair Nancy," a homebody who drank tea and knitted.

Laurel watched Michael take his usual seat and look at her with the guilty expression he had assumed since the day Dr. Spence told him that his wife's condition was untreatable, and that she would soon be dead.

Laurel liked Michael, and would have probably married him after the fair Nancy was out of the way. She was sorry for Nancy, but felt no guilt about the affair, which had started about a year before Nancy's fatal diagnosis.

Michael never suspected that standing behind him was the ghost of the one man Laurel had always loved, and whom she could never marry, a boy named Jess Parker, whose family lived in North, where they both grew up, a family her father had ruined. Laurel knew that Jess's father had threatened to kill her father, and that the only way for Jess to stay alive was to avoid her, and to get as far away from Florida as possible. So Jess had gone to New York and taken a job with a real estate firm, using his Florida connections to impress the hiring team, and had married and divorced; beyond that, she knew nothing of his life, though she would still turn and follow a receding figure in a crowd, some unknown man who walked like Jess, or carried himself in that certain sideways slanted way she loved.

Michael, who was surprisingly persistent, had pursued Laurel almost from the first day she had started at the library, ignoring her rejections and numerous sarcastic remarks in a calm but unrelenting way. A project at work had finally brought them together, and it was then that Laurel got to know Michael, who turned out to be witty and fun, if given half a chance.

Nancy, Michael complained, never gave him that chance; not through any active malice, but instead through sheer dullness of spirit. Nancy was a homebody, who liked to sit in her chair before the fire and knit caps and socks, and say absolutely nothing for hours and hours. She drank countless tiny cups of hot tea, and must have had an unusually capacious bladder, since Michael swore that Nancy would sit all day, drinking tea and knitting, and never so much as look at the bathroom door. It wasn't until much later in their relationship that Laurel realized that the woman who was dying and whom she had been jokingly calling The Fair Nancy, was, in fact, the Nancy Ebersole she and Jess had grown up with in North. After the affair with Michael had started, there had been no question of meeting his wife, and then she had gone into the hospital for the long deathwatch. As girls, they had never been great friends.

As her relationship with Michael deepened, Laurel realized that both she and Michael shared the same consuming passion; they both hated deception in all of its forms. And yet, here they were caught in the passionate deception of an adulterous affair.

Laurel discovered that Michael's affectations were his way of popping the balloons of hot air he encountered every day in the form of pompous directors, professors and pretentious scholars, who all assumed that the utility of other people's lives was directly proportional to how well they served the "truly great."

Once Laurel realized how deeply she was involved with Michael, she understood him more. At a meeting with the director, for example, he had only to look at her and give his handkerchief a tiny flick, perfectly punctuating whatever inflated pronouncement the director happened to be making at the time, and forcing Laurel to quickly turn away to stop the rising fits of laughter.

Laurel's approach was the opposite of Michael's but no less effective. She was, as Michael put it, the gray-eyed Athena of truth. She remembered everything, and was legendary for never backing down to anyone if she thought she was right, or worse, if she sensed someone was lying. She called this weaseling, and would very calmly raise objections by simply recalling in perfect detail and with a penetrating depth of understanding, the context of every statement referenced by the weaselers, and then she'd show why they were mistaken, and what, in fact, the correct interpretation was, and why it had been so interpreted by all of those involved in whatever issue was at stake. Then, she would sit calmly and stare at her opponent, saying nothing, since there was, in fact, usually nothing more to be said. Those for whom Laurel had opened the veil of reality in this way seldom returned for another look.

But Laurel, as Michael found out at the beginning of their courtship, was not easy to win. Even as they drew closer together, Laurel remained firmly in control, allowing the relationship to go only so far. Her hesitation had nothing to do with conventional morality, but rather, as Laurel put it, she had to be absolutely certain about Michael before she could make love to him.

Michael, however, suspected that even Athena might not know her own heart. He realized, of course, that he was far from what most women would think of as the ideal catch, and that his marriage to Nancy was certainly not evidence of his loving nature or a belief in any kind of continuing fidelity. But after months of rejections from Laurel, and finding himself still desperate and starved for love, he decided to force the issue. With his usual flair for the dramatic, he waited for a night of storms, and with rain pelting down and flashes of lightning illuminating the black streets, he knocked on Laurel's door, bag in hand, to say that he had told Nancy everything, and to ask if Laurel could put him up for the night.

Of course, Michael was lying, but it got him inside Laurel's apartment, and, he concluded, this was love and all was fair. Laurel, who before had only selected the choicest of men, now found herself yielding. Overcome by his willingness to risk everything, she melted, and quickly found herself naked and in bed with Michael, without quite understanding how he had persuaded her that this was what she had wanted all along.

Luckily, this turned out to be true. Michael was a tender and resourceful lover. The next morning, when he told her that he had not really left The Fair Nancy, she tried to cry a little, but he knew from the night before that she didn't really mean it, and so he held the corner of the bed sheet up in his hand like a handkerchief and began flicking his fingers. In spite of herself, she began laughing, and he took the sheet and dried her eyes and kissed her again, while she silently sent up a prayer of thanks to whatever higher powers guide lovers on their way. At this point, she might have been able to tell Michael about her first love, a boy named Jess, and about how her father had not approved of him—she didn't know why.

But behind Michael's romantic deception and Laurel's willing desire to believe him, there was something else, the real truth of their feelings about each other. And so that morning in bed, after their first night together, Laurel told Michael that he must leave Nancy, and Michael, for his part, said he was already planning the best way to bring it about. He and Nancy had long ago stopped sleeping together, and had reached the point where they could go for days and not speak. Michael had suspected that she had taken a lover, but had never been able to discover any signs of it, and, Michael swore, he would have been delighted if she had. Nancy, as far as he could tell, never went anywhere. She had chosen not to work, and remained at home, knitting caps and drinking tea and never going to the bathroom.

Always practical, Laurel asked about Nancy's money and if she had any means of support, and Michael shrugged, looking puzzled and frustrated. "Oh, she's got some money, but I don't know where it comes from. I think her mother— at least the postmark on the envelope is from North—sends her two thousand a month for living expenses." Laurel said nothing, and couldn't understand it, either. The Ebersoles had always been nothing more than poor peanut farmers. Where the two thousand a month came from, she couldn't imagine. Michael smiled and said, "It's good, in a way. She can have the house and, with her two thousand, she can do whatever she wants."

SEVEN

Nancy and Douglas

Nancy, as Michael vaguely suspected, had no need to go anywhere. Her lover, a policeman named Douglas, came to her almost every morning as soon as Michael left for work. Douglas was a brutal looking, silent man over forty, who had spotted Nancy out in the yard planting winter daisies as he drove by her house one afternoon. Glancing at her, he instinctively saw something he liked, and when he reached the end of the block, he circled around and drove back toward her house for a second look. Just before he reached Nancy's yard, he slowed the car down to a quiet glide so he could take a long, slow look at her, kneeling in the dirt, with her hands working the soil and a box of flowers on the ground nearby. He could tell she had a lush, full figure. Nancy looked up at him, tucking away a loose strand of her beautiful black hair, and giving him a slow, dreamy smile of appreciation as he passed. That was all he needed.

Douglas was not sure this was the woman he had been asked to put under surveillance, and so he pulled a photograph of Nancy out of the glove compartment, just to make sure. Scrawled on the back of the photograph was the address, with the name "Nancy Tuttle/Ebersole." Douglas wasn't sure why he had been sent to watch her; he had only been told "The Boss" wanted to know how she was doing. The Boss always meant Leon Putnam, and Douglas was simply told to "find out all you can."

Douglas drove out to the highway and began to scout the neighborhoods for a way to approach Nancy's house without being seen. It didn't take long. There was a tract of wooded land that ran along the road behind the row of houses on Nancy's block. Douglas guessed that the tract had not been sold because most of it was low wetlands, where a slow creek meandered through, and which probably rendered the land unusable for almost any kind of development. On the other side of the creek, the woods went up a hill and continued on out of sight for about a hundred yards before reaching another developed area. Douglas took out his city map and saw an access road leading into the wooded land behind Nancy's house. He drove to the spot, and found a small dirt road curving out of sight before coming to a dead end. He could park there and walk through the woods, cross the creek, and come out behind Nancy's house without being seen.

Douglas waited until the next morning, and drove by the front yard where he had watched Nancy kneeling by the box of flowers. Everything seemed normal. He went past the house and turned left toward the main road, turned left again and drove up a hill to the dirt road that led into the woods.

Douglas parked the car and walked silently back toward Nancy's house. The ground was clear beneath the trees,
and the creek was easy to cross. As he came to the edge of
the woods, he could see there was nothing to worry about.
Because of the angle of the road, Nancy's house was slightly
recessed behind the two neighboring houses, and, Douglas
thought, there would only be an instant when someone could
see him as he crossed the yard. He paused and looked for any
signs of activity. There were no dogs to worry about. Everything seemed quiet. He walked silently toward the small back
porch.

Inside, Nancy was still in her bathrobe, drinking
a fourth cup of morning tea and reading the paper at the
kitchen table. Her back was to the door, and when Douglas
knocked, she was so startled that she jumped upright in her
chair, rattling the cup in its saucer. Suddenly frightened, she
looked at the door to make sure it was locked. There was another knock, even stronger and more insistent than the first.
Nancy stood up as quietly as possible and walked on her bare
feet to the kitchen window and looked out through the cur-
tains. It was the policeman she had seen the morning before.
She studied the deep, cruel lines in his face, masked behind the
same large aviator sunglasses he was wearing when he drove
past her front yard. Nancy looked at him for what seemed like
a long time, taking in the details of his immaculate uniform
of heavy, gray wool, with the large black leather belts carefully
polished, and the brim of his Stetson hat cocked at a rakish
angle. His boots and holster gleamed in the morning sun. He
knocked again.

Nancy walked to the door, turned the lock and slid
back the deadbolt, hesitating a moment to steady her breathing before she opened the door.

Douglas looked up at her. "We've had some reports

of prowlers in the woods. Have you seen anyone?"

"No," Nancy answered. "It's very quiet here."

"Are you alone?"

"Yes. Quite alone, during the day."

"Maybe you need some protection."

Nancy's mouth opened slightly and her breath came in small, gasping spurts. Douglas waited. Her pink tongue came out and delicately wet her bottom lip and then withdrew. "I'm not sure," she said. "Perhaps you can tell me what to do, if you think I need anything, Officer . . ." Her voice trailed off.

"Everybody calls me Douglas," he said.

Nancy stepped back and held the door open. Douglas came inside. She pulled out a chair for him at the kitchen table, and with her back to him, she walked to the stove, where Michael had left the pot of fresh coffee he always made for breakfast. She fumbled around, trying to find a cup, while at the same time she loosened the ties of her gown so it would fall open.

But as she tried to pour the coffee, her hands suddenly took on a life of their own and began shaking violently. She finished pouring the coffee, and holding the cup tightly in both hands, Nancy turned and walked slowly back toward Douglas, with the cup in front of her so her gown would catch the air as she moved.

Having been sure of what would happen from the moment Nancy opened the door, Douglas, who had not bothered to sit down, watched her. Breathing even harder now, Nancy stopped in front of him like a priestess, fearfully lifting up her offering. Douglas reached out and with one hand took the cup, while he placed his other hand between her palms.

Mesmerized, Nancy watched as her fingers curled around his massive fist, squeezing his hand tighter and tighter until, finally, her own hands stopped shaking.

Without looking away from her, Douglas leaned toward the table and put the cup down. Nancy stood, unable to move, seemingly tied to him by her two hands, which had tightened around his with such force that it made her arms hurt. Eyes bulging, she stared insanely in front of her, trying to make her fingers release their grip, while Douglas, his other hand now free, reached between the open folds of the gown and pulled her toward him with a quick jerk. Nancy's legs buckled, and she collapsed against him with a little cry.

Douglas picked her up like a rag doll and walked through the house, quickly putting her down on the first bed he could find. Still sure of himself, he did nothing more than take off his boots before he pulled her gown up and placed himself between her legs. Nancy reached out, holding on to his massive black belt with both hands, and wrapping her thighs tight around him so she could feel his body sliding back and forth beneath the delicious, hairy roughness of the wool uniform.

Douglas took the long strands of her lustrous black hair in both hands and pulled, riding her expertly across the bed as she twisted beneath him. Then it was over. Not bothering to move, Nancy watched enthralled as he pulled on his boots and stood up.

"I'll use the large window upstairs," she said. "The curtain will be open if I want you to come."

He nodded, and started to leave.

"Don't ever call here on the phone," Nancy continued. And never come to the front door, and come only in the morning, after nine."

Douglas turned and looked at her. "Sure," he said. Then he was gone before she could say anything else.

When she heard the door click shut, Nancy ran to the kitchen window, watching him walk away through the winter woods until the back of his gray uniform faded out of sight like a ghost.

Nancy scanned the trees with quick, nervous glances, thinking Douglas might turn and come back. But after a moment, she realized that he had continued on up the hill, and she looked around the kitchen, trying to remember the lost world of her life thirty minutes ago, before Douglas had knocked on the back door. But her mind was a blank.

Astonished, she saw a cup of coffee on the kitchen table and took it to the sink, washed it, and then wiped the table clean. Next, she washed the coffee pot, and then the counters and the cabinets that lined the walls around the sink. Then she mopped the floor, working faster and faster until the floor was shining, only to find herself unaccountably standing in the middle of the room, tears streaming down her face. Wiping her eyes, she put away the mop and the old rags she used for cleaning. As she closed the closet door, Nancy stopped momentarily, and looked down the hall toward the guest bedroom. Something seemed to pull her in that direction.

Still in her trance, Nancy moved down the narrow passage like an automaton, examining the carpet and walls inch by inch for a boot print or a stain, any sign that might tell her what had happened. But when she reached the bedroom, and saw the twisted blankets, and the pillows on the floor where she had kicked them, the memory of those few, vivid moments came back with such violence that her heart seemed to stop, and she dropped beside the bed, leaning her head against the mattress and crying quietly for a long time.

The morning passed. Nancy's hands trailed across the bed, trying to trace the imprint their bodies had made, and thinking about the man who had surprised her. He must have come through the woods after seeing her in the yard yesterday, she thought. Why? How was it possible that she had let him come inside her house? And what would she do now? Was he dangerous? But he's a policeman, she thought, and then realized how that only made it worse. Who would believe her if she reported him? He could do anything he wanted and get away with it.

She thought about the curtain, and the signal they had agreed on. He won't really do it, she told herself. It's too big a risk for him to come a second time. He wouldn't know what kind of trap might be waiting for him.

Nancy held out for three days before the anxiety and doubt became too much for her. Then, on the third night, she opened the curtain on the window upstairs; in case Douglas came by early while she was still in bed. She kept telling herself that this was just to prove that he wouldn't come back, so she could put it out of her mind. After all, she reasoned, she couldn't go on living this way, thinking that he might show up unexpectedly at any moment.

The next morning, after Michael left the house, Nancy took her station, sitting quietly at the kitchen table and pretending to knit, like Penelope at her loom. Then, just after nine, there was a heavy, insistent knock like the one that had sounded so unexpectedly three days ago. Nancy flew to the door. When she opened it, Douglas was standing there, impassively waiting. Nancy smiled at him, unable to remember the last time she had felt so happy and light-hearted.

Later, when Nancy looked back on those first weeks with Douglas, she knew how they would appear to anyone from the outside, and how people would cringe on hearing the details of what happened that day, when Douglas came to her door for the first time; and they would ask her how she could have possibly done something so sordid.

But Nancy knew the truth; that she had become a prisoner within her own life, and that Douglas had given her the courage to think that another life might be possible. It was her life with Michael that Nancy saw as sordid. Michael had only pretended to love her. He had lied to her, in fact, and after a few weeks of marriage, she saw that all of the things that he said he liked about her, her cooking and her hunger for a beautiful home, the garden and flowers she wanted so desperately to grow and nurture with him, the long, peaceful nights together, all of these things he hated when he actually came to possess them. And every day, the rejection became more and more obvious, and the contempt in his face easier to read. She would never understand it. Why would anyone pretend to like a kind of life they hated? Nancy could never forgive Michael for his lies, and the cruelty of his rejection.

But with Douglas, Nancy felt, she was starting out clean, with no promises, and with the door open anytime he chose to leave. Fortunately, she let things move slowly at first, sensing that he wanted nothing more than to take her to bed, and, she let him know, that was fine with her. She wanted that, too. But each time, when he started to leave, Nancy would look at him and say, "Would you like some coffee before you go?" or "I just made an apple pie. Why don't you stay and have some?" And each time, she felt, there was a little more hesitation before he said "No, I have to get back," taking his hat and walking quickly away through the woods.

She wanted nothing from him except to talk. Who was this man, she wondered, and where did he live? He seemed too lonely to have a wife and a family. What had happened?

Then one day, just as he was leaving, he looked at the plate of freshly baked cookies she had placed on the table, and walked over and picked up a handful. "I like these," he said, taking a thoughtful bite. "I haven't had homemade cookies in a long time." Nancy said nothing, but smiled, stepping close and almost leaning against him as she gave him his hat. Without thinking about it, he took her in his arms, and for the first time he kissed her goodbye. It was, she thought with a smile as she watched him disappear through the woods, like coaxing a wild kitten to come closer and closer by leaving pieces of food on the ground.

After that, there were always freshly baked cookies on the table. At first, he would talk to her and not sit down, taking small careful bites from a cookie and edging away toward the door. But soon, they were sitting at the table together, sharing a pot of tea, which he preferred to coffee, Nancy was thrilled to discover, and talking about the things that had happened to him since his last visit.

Nancy listened as he talked, and when he paused, her quiet, responsive questions prompted him to go on, until, faster and faster, the events of his life came tumbling out, and he was telling her how, still almost a boy, he fled from his parents' life of poverty on an isolated farm in Maine, leaving his three brothers behind to freeze in the cold and dig rocks out of the hard, black dirt. He had learned how to keep equipment running under almost any conditions; the Maine winters and the rocky soil had taught him that. He found jobs that took him all over the world, first working oil rigs, and then joining the army. He had fought in the Middle East, he told her, and killed other men, but growing bored with the monotony of peacetime soldiering, he left the army, and without thinking about it too much, he became a policeman. And he had always lived alone, he said, taking what he wanted, and asking help from no one.

Nancy listened through it all, and from time to time, as he remembered some particular detail of his life that he had forgotten, he would almost smile, and she could see the lines in his face soften. Nancy loved him then, for all the things he had done, and for what he had suffered. And Douglas, though he did not know what name to give it, fell so in love with Nancy that, after a few weeks, he would sit down at the table first, talking as long as he could before taking her to bed; and later, there were days when he would become so engrossed in their talk that the minutes would pass unnoticed, until he would look at his watch and catch himself, giving her a hurried kiss goodbye, and saying "Later," before leaving through the back door.

The next few months, as the brief north Florida winter passed and spring came on, were the happiest days Nancy had ever known. As she and Douglas gradually shared their confidences with each other, and as Douglas learned more and more about her life, he urged her to leave Michael and make a new beginning. This was what Nancy wanted more than anything. Douglas helped her with the plans, showing her how it might be done, and even driving her around town to look for a suitable apartment. They talked obsessively now, sometimes for an hour or more, sitting at the kitchen table and holding hands as they began making arrangements for the move. In the next week or two, they both agreed, Nancy would tell Michael that she was moving out.

Once, Douglas had asked Nancy about money, and she told him that she had an inheritance that yielded about two thousand a month. She could take care of herself. She didn't want to tell Douglas any more, that the money came from a man named Leon Putnam, who had assaulted her when she was in high school, and that a young boy had witnessed it, and that her mother had used this to blackmail Leon. She had never told this to anyone, not even Michael.

A few days before she was going to tell Michael that she was leaving, Douglas stood at the back porch as usual and knocked on the door. When there was no answer, he turned the handle and went inside, only to find Nancy lying unconscious next to the stove. She was breathing quietly, so he simply wiped her face with a wet towel to bring her around.

Douglas took Nancy to the emergency room at the university hospital. Nancy made him leave her; telling him that she felt much better, and that he should go back to work. She called Michael from the hospital phone. He was in a meeting, and Nancy told someone to give him a message. By the time Michael reached the hospital, Nancy was in the middle of her examination. Two weeks later, after a long series of tests, she and Michael sat quietly in Dr. Spence's consulting room as he explained about leukemia, saying that, in Nancy's particular case, the prognosis was not optimistic.

The room was too small and too hot, and Michael, for once, used his handkerchief for what it was intended, mopping his brow and looking sideways at Nancy as the doctor droned on. For several weeks now, Nancy had suspected that she was seriously ill, and so was not surprised at the doctor's news. Michael, however, had received Nancy's message from the hospital the morning of the day he had planned to tell her that he was moving out. Never dreaming that her condition was so serious, he put off leaving until Nancy was feeling better, explaining to Laurel that he would tell Nancy about his plans as soon as the doctors knew what was wrong.

But as the slow process of diagnosis proceeded, and the news grew more and more ominous, each visit to the doctor tightened Michael's desires around his throat like a noose, until he now sat with Nancy in the consulting room, listening to Dr. Spence, and feeling like Ali Baba, whose wish has just been granted by the genie, but in a particularly nasty way he had not foreseen.

Nancy will die, he thought, and it will all be so easy.

There was no need now to tell her anything. Now, he would not even have to move out of his house. There would be no unpleasant divorce, with lawyer's fees and alimony payments. Convenience, thy name is death. And though Michael suffered as the waves of shame and guilt swept over him, he could never completely silence those voices whispering in the night: Nancy will die . . . Nancy will die . . .

Laurel watched as Michael agonized, hating what had happened to them. Of course, she and Michael wanted Nancy to get well, but it wasn't their fault that Nancy had contracted a fatal disease; no one could believe that. But even more, Laurel hated lying about it. She wanted to begin her life with Michael with everything on the table; no secrets and no regrets. Instead, she found herself gritting her teeth as Michael moved from not telling Nancy anything until she was better, to Michael not telling Nancy anything at all. And, Laurel would say to herself in exasperation, there she was, agreeing with Michael every time he changed his plans, telling him that there was nothing else they could do but remain silent. Then, in a desperate effort to still her circling mind, she would make herself sit for long moments in a chair, listening as her breath quietly moved in and out of her body.

Nancy's condition worsened. As Michael's hours nursing Nancy increased, his time with Laurel dwindled to occasional moments at work, when they might find themselves briefly alone in Laurel's office, or at lunch on a bench behind the library, hidden out of sight behind some trees, where they would sit huddled close together, sharing their sandwiches and searching each other's eyes for signs of change.

Together they waited as the spring approached, and the warmer weather opened the early buds. The rains came, and the waters washed across the streets and fields, filling the creeks, and freshening the rivers with new strength. Laurel knew that somehow she and Michael had been carried out into the flood, and were being swept along toward some uncharted destination. But engrossed in other things, she never heard the echoing chaos of the rapids that sounded in front of them, nor felt the current behind urging them on.

EIGHT

Grace

How to begin? What can I tell my two sons about Leon Putnam and how I tried to save our family? When George died, and we lost our orange groves to Leon's bank, it was all I could do to save our house and the five acres, which ran just from the blacktop in front of our house down to the lake. Leon granted us that, but I paid a heavy price for it. I would have had to pay more, if it had not been for a phone call the day Leon was coming to pick me up.

Leon wanted me, wanted me in the way powerful men want the woman of someone they have destroyed, and I said yes, I would do it, for five acres and his agreeing that this would be the only time, and that when it was over, he would never bother me and my two sons again. Looking back, I know how foolish I was to believe that Leon would keep his word, and while it is true that I never had sex with him, it is also true, to my undying shame, that I had agreed to it, and that, on the day Sarah Ebersole called me, I was waiting for Leon to come and pick me up for a trip to a motel in Palatka where, I prayed, no one would recognize me. And though I never got to the motel with Leon that day, it is also true that the way I stopped Leon was also the way Leon, years later, would use to drive Jess and Hal away from me and their home.

What would it take to satisfy a man like Leon? How many acres did he need to own, how many banks filled with money would it take, how many lives destroyed? The answer is, to some degree, the same for all of us, our desires can never be satisfied. There is always some unobtainable "more" that we all need, some bright light that we all move toward, and vainly circle around, finding that the sense of completion we thought was finally within our grasp, has receded from us once again, and that it is sitting there floating beyond us as a felt presence, invisibly drawing us toward it once again.

And the greater deception is when we think we have renounced our desires, and that it would be possible for us to turn away from them as vain or mistaken, but we have only turned inward, hating the world around us as dangerous and something to be guarded against. And out of this, without our realizing it, comes envy, which brings us out of ourselves and back into the world, but in a perverted way, making us want to seize and destroy the enjoyment of others by possessing what they have.

Who can say where our desires will lead us, since we can never really understand what they are, and in what part of our lives they have their origin. What was it that turned my hatred of Leon into something that lived inside me as my most precious possession, and why could I never grasp that, like the coins of the miser, it was just the possession of it, and not the value of the gold, that I needed more than anything, and that literally, almost overnight, I could identify my essential self, my very being, as having become the woman who hated Leon.

And even before this, I think, before my marriage and having children of my own, back into my own childhood, I had felt the need to create a person outside myself, someone who was impervious to all the demands of others, a false self that could hide and protect my real self, the real self that no one else could ever know. And when Leon threatened all of this, the self I had created and the life I had built up around it, I could feel my anger harden around me into hatred, creating an unbreakable shield that only death itself would finally penetrate.

The last thing I wanted as I waited for Leon that day was a phone call from someone as distraught as Sarah Ebersole. She needed help, and she said that my son, Hal, knew something that could help her daughter, Nancy, who'd had what we used to call a nervous breakdown. I tried to stop her from coming over, but she wouldn't listen, and fifteen minutes later she was there, with her maddened eyes staring at me, and compelling me to listen to her story.

I had just started to send Hal and Jess across the lake to play with some friends, but they were still out in the yard tossing a ball, and as Sarah talked and I began to understand what had happened that day at Laurel's graduation party, I was glad I hadn't sent them away, glad that I could see how it was all going to work out, and that Sarah and I had to move fast and find out before Leon came exactly what Hal had seen, that day at the party.

When I had heard enough of Sarah's story, I said, "Wait, we have to hurry. Leon is coming here, in fifteen minutes, half an hour at the most." Her eyes widened, but before she could say anything, I motioned for her to be quiet, and hurried to the front porch and called out for Hal. "Now, Hal!" I called, with an urgency in my voice I knew he would hear.

Hal came in with an inquisitive look on his face, probably thinking there was an errand I needed him to run, but then he saw the look on our faces, and took a quick step backward. "What's wrong?" he said.

"Mrs. Ebersole needs to talk to you," I pointed to a chair in front of us. "She needs to ask you a few questions."

Hal's eyes searched our faces for a clue about what was happening, and I could tell he had no idea what this was all about. It only took a couple of questions from Sarah to cause him to shrink back in his chair and grow rigid with fear.

"Hal, do you remember Laurel Putnam's graduation party last June?" Hal nodded, and said "Yes ma'am."

"My daughter, Nancy, was there, do you remember? She says you were there, and that you saw something happen between her and Leon Putnam, Laurel's father. Is that true?"

Hal's ashen face and strangled cry confirmed the truth of it all. "I . . . I saw . . ."

"Tell us what you saw, Hal," I said. "Was Mr. Putnam doing something to Nancy?"

"I'm not sure. He was . . ."

"Tell us, Hal. He was what?"

"He was holding her up, or something."

"How was he holding her?" Sarah said in a low whisper.

"He was pushing her up against the dock, and his arm was around her."

I knew we had to ask, and I thought it was better to come from me. "Did she have her bathing suit on?"

Hal gave a low sob, and shook his head, not looking at

us. "No, it wasn't on. It was . . ."

"It was what?"

"It was on the sand beneath her feet."

"How could you tell?"

"I had on my diving mask. I could see them underwater."

"Did Mr. Putnam see you?"

Hal just nodded his head.

"Did he say anything to you?"

"Nothing much. He cursed me, and wanted to know where I had come from, or something like that."

"And then what happened?"

Hal shrugged, and said, "Nothing happened. He got in a boat and left. That was all."

Sarah leaned forward. "Did Nancy say anything?"

Hal looked confused. "I don't think so. By the time Mr. Putnam got to the boat, she had run away."

"Was her bathing suit back on?"

"Yes, it was," Hal said simply.

I nodded to Sarah and stood up. This was enough, more than enough, I thought, to deal with Leon.

I stood up and walked Hal to the door. Jess was still out in the yard throwing the ball up in the air. "Don't ever say anything about this, not to anyone, even Jess," I said to Hal. I leaned over and took his arm, holding it tight and forcing him to look at me. "It could hurt a lot of people if you do. Do you understand?"

Hal nodded. "Yes, Ma'am."

I looked up to call to Jess, but just as I did, I could see Leon's car slowing down and turning into our driveway. I waved to Jess, who, seeing Leon's car, came over in a slow, loping run.

"Go down to the lake," I said, "Right now. Don't

come back until I call you. Go this way," I said, pointing to the side of the house that would take them away from Leon. I watched them go, and then hurried back inside and sat down next to Sarah. "Don't worry," I said. "This will work out for both of us." I could hear the front porch door open and I whispered, "Just tell him what we know, straight out."

At this time, Leon was still an imposing man. He was tall and lanky, with big ears and a large nose and mouth, and he knew how to bend other people to his will by knowing them well, by finding out about their families, relations, birthdays and, most importantly, finding out their secrets, what they wanted or needed, or were afraid of, and using all of this information during whispered conversations, where he would hold on to your arm and pull you toward him, promising to deliver a favor, or help you out. Behind all of this political acumen, however, was a voracious sexual acquisitive drive, and that made him grasp for whatever woman or piece of property that was available.

Knowing all of this, Sarah and I sat facing Leon as he walked into the room. Seeing us sitting at the table facing him, with a chair across the table waiting for him, he tried to joke.

"This looks like a meeting," Leon pulled out the chair and sat down. Then he looked at me. "I wasn't expecting company."

"Sarah wants to talk about something that happened at Laurel's graduation party." I paused and looked at Sarah.

"Nancy says you tried to . . . that you assaulted her while she was swimming out by the dock. She's had a nervous breakdown. She has nightmares and wakes up screaming at night."

"You pulled her bathing suit off," I added.

"Now how would you know that?"

"Hal saw you. You spoke to him."

For the first time, Leon's face quivered imperceptibly as he looked at me. "That's your little boy?"

"He's twelve. He knows what he saw."

"Well, no one else saw anything."

Sarah leaned forward. "Nancy told one of her friends who was there."

"Now who would that be?" Leon said.

"Never mind who it was. She saw Nancy running up from the dock. Nancy was crying."

Still calm, Leon paused as if considering something. "You know, this all seems just a little too much like a setup, to me. How long have you two been planning this?"

"I had to take Nancy to a clinic," Sarah said. "She needs serious treatment, and for a long time. I'll need two thousand a month just to meet expenses. She told the doctor everything. He believes her."

Leon paused again, then nodded. "I'll send you the money the first of every month."

It was then that I realized that I could feel Sarah's leg trembling under the table, and that my muscles were drawn so tight that I could hardly move.

Leon stood up as if to leave, then looked at me as if nothing of any consequence had been happening for the last ten minutes. As if he had not admitted to assaulting Nancy. "I'll be waiting for you out in the car. It's an hour's drive to Palatka."

I don't remember what happened next. The room seemed to go white with flashing explosions, and when they went away Leon was gone. Sarah said that I threw a vase so hard at Leon that it went sailing out the open living room door and on to the porch, before shattering against a big clay flower pot, while I kept screaming, "Leave my house, you son-of-bitch," and that as he was leaving he told Sarah, "Tell her to look out for her boys, and keep them real close."

The following week, the deed to the house and five acres came in the mail. Leon knew we had enough evidence to ruin his career, and that even if we didn't, Laurel would know and believe us. Hal and Jess, I learned later, had come in through the back porch and were listening.

NINE

The Assasins

When I was young, my mother and father lost our family farm. We raised oranges and grew peanuts, and when the weather didn't cooperate, and the debts piled up, my parents borrowed money against the land and the equipment and the house in the hopes that next year things would work out and the bank could be paid off. In our town, Leon Putnam was the bank, and finally he called the note in and demanded payment in full.

I remember that my parents had a big argument about what was happening, and that it was so violent I ran outside and stood behind a live oak in our front yard, thinking that, while I still might hear their muffled shouts, if I couldn't understand what they were saying it wouldn't scare me so much.

I walked in a circle around the tree, relentlessly counting my steps and trying not to hear what was going on; cooperating, as children have to do, in their own destruction.

Then, at about step one thousand and twenty-three, I came around the tree's enormous trunk, and saw that Leon's car, a big black Cadillac, had pulled up in our driveway, and that Leon was sitting there, looking at me through the car window, his face alive with the swift flow of thoughts and emotions as he listened to the muffled arguments coming from inside the house, while watching me and guessing at what I might do. At almost the same time, the shouting inside the house died down, and my father came out in a rush, banging open the screen door and hurrying toward me, his eyes on the ground with the same fixed stare as mine had been as I relentlessly counted my steps around the tree. I thought he didn't see me, but as he walked past, his head turned slightly and whispered with a threatening hiss, "Don't ever mention this to anybody." Then he got inside the car beside Leon and they drove away. I ran toward the road, trying to keep my father's face in sight as the car disappeared through the pines. I don't think he ever looked back.

Like a good victim, I never did tell anybody, and I guess this is one way to think about life here in this small, out of the way town, hidden under the live oaks and the slash pines, where the clear lakes reveal the depths of things with such natural ease, and how many of us have lived here for years and never told the little, disconnected bits of what we know about different things, not because we don't know, or we can't tell, but because we're afraid that if we do tell, as we have always understood, somehow, almost from the beginning, that those who love us also protect us, and that there is an acknowledged but invisible power that hovers over our lives, and that the clear lake waters which reveal such depths might also become places where we could disappear forever.

There was always danger lurking about, though at that age we didn't know it. When I was about seven, my parents gave a party down by the lake, and a lot of their friends came, but for some reason, my brother and I were the only two children there. So, in the way children have, we moved away from the adult crowd, toward a little cove about fifty yards away from our dock and the beach where my parents and their friends sat on blankets and talked quietly.

Jess was just beginning to date Laurel, if date is the right word, and he would arrange for Laurel and Nancy Ebersole to meet us at the cove. Laurel claims that she had always loved Jess, and Jess, in my opinion, always loved her, but as far as I can remember, these meetings at the cove were the first serious beginnings of what would come later. Tonight, however, Jess and I were at the cove alone.

I had lived around the water all my life, but for some reason I still had not really learned to swim, and while I am sure that my mother and father were keeping an eye on us, they were so preoccupied with their own lives, like losing the farm and deceiving Leon and the bank about the financial situation, it seemed that no one was really concerned about our getting into trouble. So we were left pretty much alone to do what we wanted. Sad.

Jess, three years older and a good swimmer, would throw out an inner tube and then swim to it, while I paddled near the shore and kicked my feet. The water in the cove was shallow, but it quickly deepened over my head if I moved out toward my brother, just a few feet away. I sat there quietly for a while, building figures out of sand and then watching them melt away as I covered them with water. I could do this, and still watch my brother as he dove under the black inner tube and surfaced inside the hole, then pulling himself up and, with a big splash, turning the tube over and swimming back toward me with strong, precise strokes.

When you can't swim, the water is always frightening, but for some reason, perhaps it was the heat of the day, or the quiet murmuring of voices from the grownups at the party, a feeling of confidence swept over me, and after watching my brother swimming toward me over and over again with such ease, I stood up and asked him, "Can I do that?"

Without pausing, Jess said, "Sure. I'll push you out to the tube and you swim back," and before I could think about the consequences, he put his arms around me and shoved me out toward the tube, just a few feet away. In shock, I went under for an instant before bobbing up. I tried to breathe, and instead of air, sucked in mouthfuls of water. Fortunately, the tube was almost close enough to grab, and with my arms flailing the water like a bird flapping its wings, I was able to lunge toward the tube and get an arm around it. I clung to the tube, gagging as I tried to breathe, and paralyzed by the insight that I was on the water alone. I looked back at my brother, who smiled and said, "Great. Now swim back." Even now, years later, I don't think Jess understands how terrified I was.

Another story about my brother Jess and me goes like this. We used to play a game called "Assassins." We would dress up in homemade camouflage outfits, and just at dusk we would go out and pretend to stalk bank robbers who knew we could identify them, and were coming for us in the cars that came by on the lonely blacktop road that ran by our house. I would have a BB gun and Jess would have my grandfather's old squirrel rifle. The game was to see how close we could get to the road without the people in the passing cars seeing us. Jess was the captain, and I was the sergeant.

On this particular night, Jess was kneeling by the side of the road, listening for approaching cars. I was hiding behind a bush. After a long wait, Jess heard a car approaching, and trotted back to where I was waiting. He looked at me, and then he smiled. "Take cover," was all he said.

We waited, hidden in the deep brush beside the road as a car approached. We had heard the tires on the road long before we could see the headlights. The car rounded the curve to our right, coming toward us from about a hundred yards away.

Just past us, on the left, a dirt road came in, intersecting with the black top of the small country road where we were waiting. The car passed us, and we looked at each other and smiled, congratulating ourselves on once again not being discovered. Then, astonishingly, the car slowed and pulled into the intersection where the two roads met, then stopped, with the lights still on and the engine idling. I guessed a late model Ford sedan. Except for the car's headlights, it was pitch black, and I tensed up, fearful that we had finally been spotted. Jess held up his palm, signaling for silence. Just a reflex, I thought. We both knew it was time to be quiet. I did a check in my mind, wiggling my finger to make sure it was well away from the trigger of my imaginary Savage 360. My Colt ,45 was in my belt, pressing into my back.

Two men got out of the car and moved into the glare of the headlights. One was a tall black man wearing jeans and a sweatshirt with a hood pulled back on his shoulders. The other was a white man, Leon Putnam. The black man seemed unsure of what he was doing. He scuffed his feet and they began talking furiously for a moment, then the white man took out a flashlight and moved off into the woods on the other side of the road. I could follow his movements by just watching the beam of light.

The black man, waiting calmly, pulled out a gun and leaned against the car. If he means business, I thought, Leon, moving through the woods with the flashlight, didn't have a chance. We watched the winking light as it moved through the woods and with a shock, I realized that Leon was heading toward our house. Then the winking light stopped, and Leon started moving back toward the road.

What to do? I imagined a gunfight that would settle everything and save our home. Jess had a night scope, and I could see him sighting up. We waited. If he shot the black dude, he could save Leon's life. I didn't think Jess would do that. Even though the nearest house was a couple of miles away, somebody might be out late and hear the shot. Then again, we didn't know why they were there so late at night. We knew Leon was the bad guy who had taken our orange grove. He looked like he didn't know what he was doing, and maybe he was drunk and would turn against us if he knew we were there. The black guy was more dangerous.

We could take one or both of them out. We were thinking like TV criminals, not like boys in Florida, trying to play games that would take our minds off what was happening to our lives. The car was a problem—cars were hard to hide, and people always came looking for them. In the game we had created, we had decided long ago not to risk cars. This was why we needed to call it quits for the night, go home and pretend everything was fine. We could make a big circle and come up behind the house. So we went back toward the lake, and followed it up to our house. We had always pretended we could live in the woods. We were survivalists. As we left, I looked back toward the woods where the light from the flashlight was still winking, seeming to move in a circle, as if Leon wasn't sure of where he was going. Drunk, we were now sure.

TEN

The Deep Truth

My family had lived in Florida for generations; at least that is what I grew up hearing. But as a boy, I had never understood what being Southern meant. In spite of the Civil Rights Movement, most schools were still segregated—mostly black public schools and all white-flight private academies.

Now, when I talk to Dr. Cranston about it, that is, about growing up in North, my first memories are of slashed pines, palmettos and lakes so clear you can drink the water, which we did.

As boys we could roam freely around the lakes, paddling our old fishing boats and stopping off at the docks where our friends lived. Every lake was different, and our lake, Lake Rosa, was about a mile and a half across and in our eyes was unique by having what we called the gator pond.

If you did not know it was there you would miss the gator pond, because it was hidden by what seemed the end of the lake on that side, that is the water had spilled over a slightly higher stretch of land that was almost like a dam. The water suddenly became very shallow, and to reach the gator pond we had to get out of our boats and push them, wading across this narrow shallow area to the other side of the dam, where the water suddenly got deeper again, forming a small pond that was semi-detached from the main body of the lake. I never actually saw an alligator in our lake, but people who live close to the gator pond said they could hear gators roaring there at night. My guess is that the gators had long ago been hunted out, and that if any survived it would be in a place like the gator pond.

There were probably ten or twelve houses around the lake, and with our friends we probably visited most of them. Mrs. Ebersole was always glad to see us and would let us fish and swim from her dock, and if we happened not to bring our bathing suits, she would let us swim buck.

There were two houses that we never stopped at, one belonged to Bobby Bushway, a rich northern man who invented the peanut roasting machines that used to be found at the front of the local dime stores, stores that have long since disappeared, together with Mr. Bushway's peanut roasting machines.

As a boy, Mr. Bushway's house seemed like a mysterious castle, but as a teenager, I had a summer job mowing his grass once a week, and the mystery vanished as I mowed what seemed to be an endless lawn. The other house belonged to Colonel Fisher. His wife, Mrs. Fisher, lived there with her young son Hugh, who was our age, and once in a while Mrs.

Fisher would invite us in for gingerbread cookies. Her son, Hugh, always wore khaki shorts and a T-shirt and once told me his full name was Hugh Alfred Fletcher McClellan Fisher. I would later learn that the McClellan was from the Civil War general's family, who was related to the Fishers in some way. Colonel Fisher had attended West Point, and as far as I could tell, so had all his male ancestors. He had an older son, Max, who was enrolled at West Point at the time I was growing up.

As far as I could tell Colonel Fisher never came home, and Mrs. Fisher lived there alone with her son Hugh. It was Mrs. Fisher who introduced me to opera and the Civil War. My mother liked to read and once a month she took us to the county library in Gainesville. I started voraciously reading things like the Tarzan books and the Hardy Boys.

One day, when we had been invited in for cookies, Mrs. Fisher was listening to some music on the radio. I thought it was beautiful and asked her what it was. She said it was the Metropolitan Opera broadcast that she liked to listen to every Saturday. I started listening and was entranced. Of course, I could not understand the Italian, but she filled me in on what was happening in the story. Jess and Hugh finished their cookies and went back to jumping off the dock, while I stayed with Mrs. Fisher and listened to the opera.

I won't say that I was a regular visitor, but I did come a lot with Jess and Hugh, and one day I saw a book on the table by a man named Bruce Catton. The book looked new and the jacket had a picture of some kind of battle, and I asked her what it was about. Mrs. Fisher, who I later learned was from an old Southern family, smiled and said, "Why, it's about the war."

"You mean Korea?" I asked.

Mrs. Fisher's eyes widened. "No, of course not. It's about the Civil War, our Civil War." She paused, and said

"You do know what that is, don't you?"

"No, not really," I answered truthfully, "but I've heard about it."

This time, Mrs. Fisher smiled. Then she asked, "Well, why don't you read about it?" She paused, and then said, "Do you like to read?"

"I read all the time. I love it," I said, with a little bravado in my voice. "My mother takes us to the library in Gainesville once a month."

Mrs. Fisher picked up the book and handed it to me and said, "Why don't you take this and read it?"

I took the book with both hands as if she were handing me a treasure, which in a way it was. But like all treasures, it came with a price, and the price was knowledge, for, to my amazement, I began to read that Americans had once fought and killed each other, and at ten years old, this was something I simply could not comprehend.

So, like all children, I began my real education by learning that some people can call something good that other people can think of as evil, and that in order to find out the real truth about this terrible war, I began, with Mrs. Fisher's help, to read every book about the Civil War that I could lay my hands on, impelled by the belief that if I read enough I would finally understand the real truth about the war. Not surprisingly, at the end, I came to understand that the truth depended on where you stood.

Colonel Fisher had acquired an enormous library of military history, and it was all housed in an upstairs room. Mrs. Fisher allowed me to take out one book and keep it for two weeks. The titles still run through my mind: *The Life of Billy Yank*, and *The Life of Johnny Reb*, *The Blue and the Gray*, *Lee's Lieutenants*, as well as volume after volume on the great individual battles of the war.

I think it was this deeper understanding that I learned from reading Civil War history at such an early age that allowed me to deal with what I saw that night as, swimming underwater, I could see Leon groping between Nancy Ebersole's legs. I began to understand that people do bad things and that, given the right circumstances, it can come out in all of us.

I often wonder if Mrs. Fisher knew what she was doing when she handed me that first book, and I remember that little smile on her face as I took the book from her, and I believe that she did know, and by handing me that first book she was saying, "Grow up, little boy, and be a man."

Mrs. Fisher always wore a silk Japanese house coat with a pattern of blue and white flowers wound around it. After my first two or three visits to check out a book she would simply point upstairs and let me go browse through Colonel Fisher's library on my own. I would come downstairs and find her sitting in the darkened living room, listening intently to the opera, her head tilted slightly downward and smoking cigarettes while sipping on a cup of coffee laced, I would find out later, with whiskey.

I would pause and say, "Thank you, Mrs. Fisher."

She would look up at me for a moment, as if she were trying to gauge how much I was really understanding of what I was reading. Then she would almost smile and say, "You're welcome, Hal," before she looked away.

It was about a year after I started visiting Mrs. Fisher, when I had been away to some Boy Scout camp for a week, that I paddled over to pick up another book. There was always a rope hanging from the dock to tie up your boat, and after securing my boat, I turned toward the house, only to see that all the windows and doors were boarded up. I would learn from Jess that Hugh had been enrolled in a boarding school in Massachusetts, and that Mrs. Fisher had moved to Germany to be with the Colonel. I never saw them again, though Jess heard later that Mrs. Fisher's other son, the one who was in West Point, had been killed in Vietnam a few years after graduating.

About the same time that the Fisher's left, the Bushways broke up in a messy divorce. It seems that Mrs. Bushway found another woman nibbling away at Bobby's peanut machine fortune. Evidently, he was rich enough to give his wife a big settlement and still have a lot of peanuts left over.

Suddenly, there were two fairly large vacant houses on our lake. It didn't come as a big surprise when we learned that Leon had bought them both. Leon took the opportunity to move one of his mistresses in to the Fisher house, and give the other to Mutt Cox, his long-time handyman and general fixer. The word was that when Leon wanted a stick of gum Mutt would go out and get it for him.

Mutt was there with Leon almost to the end, but when, after Leon's stroke, Laurel discovered that the deed to the house was still in Leon's name, Mutt had to go.

Mutt was smart enough not to cause trouble, and mentioned to Laurel that Leon had a big vacant house on the other side of Lake Santa Fe, and that he would be glad to look after it until Laurel decided what to do.

I think what I am feeling is not something like nostalgia, but something even deeper than that. I did feel that sense of return to North and being able to see it as if viewing two separate worlds, the world of my childhood with my Mother calling us in to supper, and the memories of school and our group of friends, while at the same time there was the North of Leon Putnam now sitting in his chair dead, the world of Sheriff Moses and the divers, the world of North with Spiros and Marty as part of it.

Perhaps the world each of us inhabits is like this, a world divided into a darkness where things are never what they seem and where hidden forces can reach out and strike you without warning, and on top of this world is the daylight world of sunshine that is always filled with objects we can identify and know and love.

As a child, I was terrified when the boundaries between these two worlds disappeared. In the world of North where I grew up, the deep South world of Georgia and Alabama that had migrated into North Florida, you needed to identify the signs of this dark world that were around you everywhere like fragments of a lost civilization.

It was always interesting to meet people from other parts of the country and see how they reacted to this new world around them. Once, a family from New Hampshire moved to North and lived for a time next to us on our lake. The father was an economics professor, Josiah Lowell, and he taught economics at the University. Jess and I became close friends with their two sons, Johnny and Kippy.

My mother's brother, Uncle Edward, delighted in showing strangers the local sites, and one day Uncle Edward came driving up in his big maroon Packard sedan to deliver some homemade pork sausage that he had brought back from South Carolina where some of our distant relatives still lived. Jess and I were outside playing with the Lowell boys and we ran over to his car with our new friends and introduced them to Uncle Edward, who said hello and that he was glad to meet young people from New Hampshire, a state he had always wanted to visit.

After going in to visit with my mother and deliver the sausage, Uncle Edward came back outside and motioned to us. "I'm on my way to visit Aunt Ethel, and your mother says you can all go with me. I called ahead and she wants to have us all to dinner. This might be the best meal you'll ever have."

This was all very mysterious and exciting. I remembered meeting Aunt Ethel once at a funeral, but she was really no more than a vague image of an old lady with gray hair in a black dress. We drove for what seemed a long time on winding black top roads, and then turned on to a sandy dirt road that was really nothing more than a track of sand that wound through groves of live oaks.

Aunt Ethel's house sat on a lake by itself, and as we got out of the car it seemed that we were in another world totally isolated from all that we knew as familiar and safe. Aunt Ethel stood on the porch waiting for us to come in, and as we said hello, she seemed genuinely delighted to see us. Uncle Edward gave her the package of sausage wrapped in white butcher's paper with her name on it and said, "Lucy made me promise to give you this sausage." Then he looked at us and said, "I've told these boys you would have lunch ready for us when we got here."

Aunt Ethel motioned to Jess, as the oldest, and said "Come with me." We were on a large front porch, which was screened in and faced the small lake nearby. There was a long table at one end and after a moment Jess came back with a large pitcher of iced tea and some glasses.

We sat drinking the cold tea while Uncle Edward filled us in. "That's Lake Angelo," he said, pointing toward the small lake. "Ethel and her husband Tom, who died just after Jess was born, moved here right after they were married."

We sat quietly for another few moments and then Aunt Ethel called out, "Jess, come back in here and help me bring this food to the table."

Jess jumped up and went back inside and Uncle Edward stood up and said, "Let's take our chairs over to the table and see what else needs to be done." We carried the chairs er to the table and Uncle Edward disappeared inside.

It was, as Uncle Edward promised, the best meal I ever had. There was country ham, sliced paper thin, fried chicken, green beans, rice and gravy, and light, fluffy biscuits brown at the top. The Lowell boys had never had collard greens but seemed to relish them the way we did. At the end there was a pound cake flavored by just a hint of almonds. Aunt Ethel apologized for not having vanilla ice cream to go with the cake.

After finishing the meal, we sat for a moment in an appreciative silence, until Uncle Edward said, "Ethel, Johnny and Kippy have come all the way from New Hampshire to live in North, about two miles down the road from Grace. Their father teaches at the University."

Aunt Ethel looked at Johnny and Kippy for a moment in an interested but remote way, as if they were some kind of foreign insect she had never seen, while they sat there looking back at her with bright, expectant faces, and then she leaned forward, looking, at Uncle Edward for a moment, and said "They're not nigger lovers, are they?"

Uncle Edward laughed, and said "You don't have to worry about that, Ethel. These boys know how to behave."

Jess kicked me under the table, which, I knew, was a warning for me not to say anything. Johnny and Kippy sat with their faces flushed, leaning back in their chairs and not sure exactly what had happened.

Later, I would ask my mother why we never saw the Lowell boys anymore, and she would just laugh and say, "I'm sure we'll see them again soon." But we never did.

I think that to a boy of seven or eight, this sense of a hidden world with unspoken rules about how to behave is what makes us so often remain silent when they suddenly appear out of that dark world of invisible objects we cannot see, and that these rules have just as much reality as the tree that stood outside my window as a boy, a dark shadow always lurking in my dreams. It was this world that I could not see or touch that caused me to remain silent that night when I saw Leon attack Nancy Ebersole.

ELEVEN

On the Dock

Fortunately, one of the Governor's aides had called Reverend Stickles before the service and indicated that the Governor could not stay long. We soon found ourselves outside, getting in our cars and driving over to the Baptist Church for the graveside service. Following protocol, Laurel had Reverend Stickles announce that the family (meaning Laurel in this case) hoped that everyone would come by "the home" on Lake Serena, where there would be food and a chance to visit with each other and remember Leon. The Governor excused himself, citing pressing matters of state, and he was soon streaking back to Tallahassee on the fancy jet provided by the taxpayers. But Laurel, as her mother Lila had been before her, was as popular as Leon was feared, and quite a number of us found ourselves in the yard by the lake, talking about old times and drinking what was, four days ago, Leon's whiskey.

People I hadn't seen in years were moving around me, and I felt confused, as if I were talking to the phantoms of a past life that had a strange coexistence with the present, and that they had always been there, just that I couldn't see them until today. My head swirled from the whiskey, and I went out on the dock, where a small group of what looked like people about my age were talking.

"Hello, Hal," one of the women said, turning toward me. "It's been a long time."

It was Joyce Ebersole. Nancy's sister. We had not seen each other since graduating from high school, and she had married and moved away. I had no idea why she was back for Leon's funeral.

The people with her on the dock excused themselves, and began walking toward the house to say goodbye to Laurel. Joyce smiled up at me. We looked at each other for a moment, and after the usual exchanges, I asked if she were here just for the funeral, or if she would be staying longer.

"I'm imposing on my sister now," she said, but I'll be staying, I suppose, at least for a while. You know the routine. When the kids grow up, you get a divorce and move back home."

I remembered she had a sister, quite a bit older, and said, "Where does your sister live?" Joyce smiled with a funny expression on her face, and pointed toward the lake.

"Here she comes," she replied. "You can ask her."

I looked where she was pointing and saw a woman in a canoe pulling away from the next dock down the lake. She was good with her paddle, and Joyce and I watched as the canoe came gliding toward us. I was trying to remember her name, but then her name came to me. The dock seemed to give a little under my feet. I hesitated, strangely elated as the pieces clicked into place. So the Mrs. Johnson in the newspaper report was Joyce, and Nancy's older sister, Irene, was the woman who hadn't come over to check on Leon the day he was killed. "So you're Joyce Goodman, now," I said, not as a question but a statement of fact.

Joyce looked at me and laughed, knowing that I had figured out the connections. "Yes, of course, I'm the nurse who left Leon and went to Palatka." Then she looked toward the canoe. "And that's Irene, my sister, Leon's neighbor. She's Irene Johnson now, and married, with two grown children. She was four or five grades ahead of me in school. She wasn't around too much when we were growing up."

The canoe was drawing closer, and I could almost feel the water beneath the dock, still holding the long-ago fear of Nancy's desperation as Leon assaulted her. Now, Leon was dead, and here I was talking to one of Nancy's sisters, and watching the other one paddle toward us in a canoe. I took another long swallow of Leon's whiskey.

"I never thought about fate much," I said, looking at Joyce and then toward Irene.

Joyce nodded in a matter-of-fact sort of way. "I wondered about that, and what you might be thinking. Laurel and the sheriff think Leon would still be alive if Irene had gone over to his house, after I had left. She paused. "I guess we did have a motive, didn't we?"

The canoe was closer now. Joyce dropped her voice and continued. "It was years before I stopped dreaming about it . . . what happened that night. I could never tell anybody. Laurel was one of my best friends. It would have killed her."

"So you had to suffer."

"Doesn't everybody."

"I don't think Leon suffered too much. And whoever killed him did him a favor. He was a mess at the end."

"Good," Joyce said. She paused. "Did you ever tell anybody?"

"No," I said, lying.

"Not even Jess?"

"No." I said, with another lie.

"I didn't think you did. You were probably as scared as I was."

"I was too young to be scared."

"Leon had a real nasty streak in him. We were both lucky."

I had never thought about it that way, but I knew Joyce was right. We were both lucky.

The canoe was almost at the dock now, and with a deft stab of her paddle, Irene slowed it down and sent the bow around so the canoe was broadside to us and pointing back out toward the center of the lake. She was a steady looking woman with salt and pepper hair under a big straw hat. She looked at Joyce and smiled.

"I'm off for a quick spin. Will you be home for supper?"

"You go ahead. I'll be here for a few more minutes and then start back."

"Everything is on the counter by the sink. Just heat up whatever you want." Irene lifted her paddle.

"This is Hal Parker, Irene. You remember him."

Irene looked at me and smiled. "You waved at me this morning. I saw you on the dock watching the divers. I guess they didn't find anything, or we would have heard about it by now."

"That's right. They didn't find anything," I said.

The breeze pushed the canoe toward the dock until it

was just below us. I looked down at Irene. I could see something like a metal pipe in the bottom of the canoe, wrapped
up in what seemed to be an old towel. Irene smiled up at me.

"That's my new anchor," she said. "But I don't think
it's a very good one."

Before we could say anything more, she was pushing
away from us, sending the canoe back out into the lake with
quick economical strokes. Without turning, she yelled, "Nice
to see you, Hal. Have fun."

The canoe moved smoothly away, while at the same
time I grew more and more agitated. I turned to Joyce.

"Were you with Irene when Leon was killed?"

"Does it matter?" Joyce said evenly.

"No," I said, not sure what my answer would be until
I said it. "No, it doesn't matter."

Joyce looked at me, knowing what I was thinking.

"And I wasn't over here killing Leon, either," she said.
"Though I wish I had been. Sooner or later, somebody was
going to do it. I'm just sorry it took so long."

She laughed, as if delighted to finally be able to speak
out loud what half the people in the county must have thought
over the years.

"Isn't that a terrible thing to say?" she said in a teasing
way, giving me a wink.

Joyce's eyes flashed, and they seemed to illuminate
something that had been hidden in both of us without our realizing it. I could see another Joyce coming back to life, growing clearer now as she stood before me on the dock, as if
coming out of the shadows, the Joyce I used to know before
Leon caught her sister, that night in the water.

We moved closer, as if we both felt Nancy's presence
at the same time, the laughing, high-spirited Nancy who had
been attacked by Leon in the water just below us, and now

she was reaching up toward the light, rising out of the water almost whole and complete again, that young girl in the bright two-piece bathing suit we had lost.

"It's not that easy," Joyce said. "I wish it were. But you can never stop remembering. I go for days and think that what happened to Nancy is finally behind me, and then one day, walking down the street, or waiting for the phone to ring, all of the anger and the fear come back again. It's like being chased by a wild dog. Just when you think he's gone, you hear him behind you, and you know that he will always be there, and that you'll be running for the rest of your life."

"Maybe now, with Leon dead, things will get better."

"That would be nice, wouldn't it," Joyce said, in a way that told me she knew I didn't really believe in the comfort I was offering her either.

"Hal."

"What is it?"

"No one else knows what Leon did to Nancy that night. If the police found out, Irene and I would have to answer a lot more questions.

"Don't worry," I said. "I was too far away. It was getting dark, and I could not really see what was happening." I paused, hoping my lie sounded convincing. "But what about the girl that ran down to the dock?" I asked. "The one Nancy talked to that night."

"I think Nancy made up some story about Leon being drunk and yelling at her."

"Did the other girl believe Nancy?"

"It doesn't matter if she did or not. That's all Nancy ever told her."

I'm sure Joyce knew I was lying when I said I had not seen anything. I mean, Nancy must have told her mother everything, and Joyce would know that if the real story hadn't come out by now, it never would. She was probably right to be worried, though. One of the puzzling things about Leon's murder was that there was no motive, in the sense of an immediate incident that might have caused someone to kill him—an old lecherous crook in a wheel chair—but there were plenty of grudges that had never been settled, hatreds that had been around for years, and that were probably beyond counting.

Joyce turned and stood looking back at the house and I turned with her. There were just a few guests left, and they were moving away from Laurel and Jess as they said goodbye.

"I need to say goodbye, too," Joyce said in an abrupt way. "So long, Hal. Maybe I'll see you again before you leave."

"That would be nice," I said. We went through one of those half hugs that people give when they've grown up together, but haven't seen each other since they left home, years ago. Joyce turned, and I watched her walking back to the house. She and Laurel embraced, and then talked briefly as a condolence and a thank-you were exchanged. That embrace should have shocked me, but it didn't. Southerners have a high tolerance for hiding evil behind conventional manners. I watched as Joyce disappeared around the side of the house, looking for her car, I supposed.

I turned and took one last look at the lake. I was surprised to see Irene Johnson's canoe about two hundred yards away. The canoe wasn't moving, and I could just make out Irene's profile. She seemed to be bent over and looking for something around her feet. After a moment, I could see her lift some kind of object up, and then hold it over the side of the boat and drop it in the water. I thought it might be her anchor, but then she started paddling off, turning the canoe toward the shore and the dock in front of her house. If what she dropped in the water was the anchor, it sure wasn't attached to her boat. But then I thought that maybe it wasn't an anchor, but something else, something that she didn't want the divers to find, and that she had dropped it in the deep water of the lake, where it would never be found.

I put these thoughts away as I walked back toward the house. Jess and Laurel were standing arm in arm as they waved goodbye to the last of the guests. Most of the people who came by after the funeral were strangers, at least to me. Now, in North, the place where I grew up, I was the one who was out of place, the one they looked at sideways and whispered "Do we know him?"

Jess and Laurel turned toward me and waved, and I waved back. I was glad for both of them. Jess, I had come to learn, was leaving his job in Georgia, and was coming back to North. With Leon dead, he could marry Laurel and they could make a new life together. Laurel now had plenty of money, or so we all assumed, and Jess had always wanted to develop lakefront communities around the many lakes that filled up this part of Florida. Jess was smart, and had plenty of connections, and so did Laurel. I didn't doubt that they would pull it off.

For a moment, I felt a sense of relief as the idea of North without Leon Putnam began to become a reality in my mind, and, without thinking, I walked up to Laurel and gave her a hug, and remarked how it was nice that so many people came by, and then I said how it was wonderful that she had so many good friends. Laurel's face turned expressionless, and she stepped back and said, in a formal way that corrected me, that most of the people who were there were good friends of her father's and that they were all very kind and thoughtful in remembering how much Leon had done for his state and his community.

I knew immediately that I had made a mistake, and I

understood exactly what Laurel meant. This part of Florida was, after all, still the South with a capital letter, and family appearances came first.

I tried to pull my hand out of the flames, and murmured that of course we all took it for granted that Leon was a person whose place it would be impossible to fill, and all I had meant was that it was good to know so many of them were paying their respects.

Jess then jumped in and gave Laurel a tight hug, and said, "Hal is right, it is a good thing for you to have neighbors."

Laurel seemed to relax a little, and said that she was sure we were right, but as she said it, I noticed that she turned her head away from Jess, and gave me a sharp look that said, "Don't step out of line again." Of course, I had been well trained in local matters and understood her perfectly. The mistake was mine, and I didn't mind at all.

There was a brief silence, and Jess said, "Let's have a final drink to wind things up," and, relieved, I said that I could use another bourbon. As we walked toward the house, Jess asked, "Did you talk with any old friends?"

"The two Ebersole sisters," I said. "You remember? Joyce and Irene."

I could see that this registered with Jess, though Laurel was silent as Jess opened the door for her and we went inside.

I know a man who believes that God died in 1957 and that his body was found in a motel room somewhere in Alabama. This man says that he suffers from severe disorientation, as if the world he grew up in had suddenly been replaced by another world that he didn't understand. Driving around North is like that for me, although, I suppose, my case is not so severe. Still, the things I notice cause me to jerk my head, as if I needed to refocus my eyes. There will always be change. I know that, and the new café in town trying to be trendy, with its checkered tablecloths, and gourmet coffee, doesn't surprise me. I don't miss the old rancid pot of Maxwell House left on the burner all day, and the smell of hot grease gone bad. But the "Gas, Guns, and Ammo" signs at multi-pump filling stations make me feel estranged from the town I grew up in. I remember once when I was in the sixth grade, when my brother Jess and Tommy Whitmire, both juniors, came to school to show off Tommy's new shotgun that was lying on the back seat of Tommy's old black Chevy pickup. It was a big event, and at luncheon recess all the boys rushed over to take a look. Nobody thought anything about it. Now, guns are everywhere, but bringing one to school would get you arrested. The man who pulls up beside you at a red light might be angry enough to blow you away if he doesn't like the way you look.

That was the thing about Leon's murder. It wasn't just an impulsive outburst; whoever did it planned it out, and it was up close and personal. It was a real, old-fashioned murder, by somebody who had a grudge, and who decided to act on it. Then again, maybe it was just money and power. Maybe Leon just got in the way of the wrong person, someone who wanted a piece of land that Leon owned, and that Leon wouldn't sell.

Last night, before I went to sleep in the bedroom I shared with Jess as a child, there was a song playing on the radio, a song that was mournful and unending, about Willie the Weeper, the chimney sweeper, a poor man who took a lot of dope. In the song, Willie dreams of meeting a lot of famous people, and, as the song says, the first person he meets is the Queen of Belgium, who was enormously powerful and rich: *She had a million dollars all in nickels and dimes\She knew 'cause she counted them a million times*. Leon was like that. You got the feeling that he knew everything about you, how much money you had and how you earned it, who your family was and how much land they owned, and that he wanted to know this in case he ever needed to take some of it from you. And that once he took what he wanted, he would never let it go.

I was thinking about this the afternoon of Leon's funeral, as Laurel and Jess were saying goodbye to the last visitors, who solemnly gave Laurel a hug and then turned to leave. Standing on Leon's porch, you could see Laurel's new house next door on one side, and about fifty yards away on the other side of Leon's house was the home of the neighbor who was supposed to be watching Leon's place while the nurse was away.

After the meetings on the dock, I knew that the nurse and the neighbor were the two surviving Ebersole sisters, and that my meeting with them coexisted now, and perhaps even completed, at least in my mind, that earlier happening, when Leon had raped Nancy Ebersole. All of these things coming together gave me a shiver, and I knew that I was feeling what horror film buffs call the presence of the uncanny, the dimension of the undead.

I heard a cough, and then Jess calling my name, "Come on Hal, for God's sake," as he waited, holding the door open for me to go inside. I followed Laurel, who was in the hallway.

"Stop daydreaming," she said impatiently, and turned away. I followed her into the spacious front room that faced the lake. There was a large plate glass window, with a sofa and side tables against the walls, and a leather covered recliner chair sitting in front of it, facing out toward the lake, and I intuitively knew that this was probably where Leon was sitting when he was killed. I couldn't help staring at the chair and the carpet. Jess gave Laurel's hand a squeeze and said, "You go ahead. We can wait here." Jess's voice jerked me back into the present. It wasn't until later that night, as I got ready for bed, that I realized that I had been unconsciously looking at the chair and the carpet for signs of blood.

Laurel walked quickly over to the kitchen area, past the divider counters that separated it from the living room, and started opening the cabinet doors, evidently looking for something. After a moment, she stopped and looked back at Jess. "I don't see it," she said, her voice rising with an almost desperate tone. Jess stayed calm, and said "Try the bathroom." Laurel shook her head, annoyed. "No, I wouldn't put them in there." She stood for a moment, looking at us, and then opened a couple of drawers that were in the divider, stopped, and then looked at Jess with a smile. "I remember now," she said. "I hid it in my old bedroom just before I left for the service."

Laurel disappeared down the hall. Jess and I stood quietly for a moment, and I slowly turned and looked at the recliner chair, where it sat as a silent witness, as if looking out the window at something no one else could see. Without realizing it, I heard myself saying, as if I were talking to the chair, "So . . . this is where it all happened." There was a crack and ringing in my ears as Jess slapped me, hard, and I found myself looking into his bulging eyes as he grabbed my shoulders. His face was contorted with anger, the way it had been that morning long ago when he picked up the kitchen knife. Then he slowly let go of my shoulders and looked up at the ceiling. "Jesus, Hal. Only you would say something like that. Keep your voice down, and don't mention anything about Leon." I gave him my crooked, little brother grin and murmured, "I know . . . Sorry."

Laurel came striding back into the room, holding up a burlap bag and smiling at Jess. "Got it," was all she said. "Great," Jess said and then looked at me. "Just some stuff we need to help secure Leon's house tomorrow."

"Is it that complicated?"

"You have no idea," Jess said. "Leon had so much security built in to this place we have to go over to Laurel's and figure it out. Not to mention his storage garage in Talla-hassee."

Laurel gave me a smile. "Let's go over to my place, Hal, and have a drink."

I watched them for a few moments as they went from room to room checking all the doors and windows, and setting the security alarms.

Back out on the porch they turned and looked at me and Laurel said, "Are you coming?"

"It's been a long day for everybody," I said. "I need to head back and make a few calls to the office."

TWELVE

The New Couple at the Fire

Two days after Leon's funeral, things had calmed down enough for me to make some real progress on the packing and moving at Mother's house. Jess had called, and asked me to come over and help move some of Laurel's furniture that she had in storage. After filling up two small moving trucks from a local storage place that rented out units, I was ready to head back home, and said goodnight, declining their invitation to stay for dinner. I had to pass Leon's house, and that was when things started happening, things that you don't expect and that you can't plan for.

Irene Johnson must have seen the fire about the same time I did. I had just left Jess and Laurel as they finished up arranging the furniture we had brought in, and was aimlessly driving around, thinking about where I had found the photo-graph with Leon standing on the platform in Palatka.

I could see the lights shining from the houses on the lake, and yes, I was not sure where I was, and ruefully admit-ted to myself that I was actually getting lost in North. It was like seeing an old friend who has changed and you're not sure why. When I was a boy, there were not as many lights to see, and I could name most of the families who lived in houses behind those lights. How many of those families were left now? Not many, I thought.

Looking around, I began to recognize a few familiar landmarks, and realized I was passing the driveway that led down to Leon's house. Irene, who could look out her back window and see Leon's house, said she had just turned off her TV after watching a movie, when she saw a flickering light through the trees and knew that something was wrong. This must have been just about the same time I was driving past Leon's house on the hard surfaced road. I slowed down to a dead stop and watched the strange looking light inside the house for a moment before it dawned on me that a fire must have started.

At about the same time, Irene said, she was yelling at her sister Joyce to get up, and without waiting, Irene jumped in her old pickup and headed for Leon's house on the sandy back road that ran from house to house around the lake, while calling 911 to report the fire.

Things were happening so fast that I am still not sure if I reached Leon's first, or if Irene was there waiting for me. It didn't register at the time, but it became an important fact, in my mind, at least. Irene swears that I was at Leon's house when she drove up, and for some reason, I thought she was there first. I remember walking over to where Irene was stand-ing at the same time Sheriff Moses came roaring up and told us to move back away from the house. He then asked how long we had been there, and I said we had just arrived, and Irene said that she came just after me. I hesitated and didn't contradict her, and she repeated that we had both got there at about the same time.

Irene's truck was too close to the house, and so she backed it up away from the flames that were starting to shoot out of the windows. The three of us stood there watching the fire and backing away from the heat. There was really nothing else to do, since there was no possibility of our doing anything to stop the fire, as it spread through the first floor, and then with a sudden whoosh, it moved up to the second floor and then the roof.

About two or three minutes later a state police car pulled up with all the lights flashing. The state trooper stayed in the car, and I could see he was on his car radio and probably telling the people at the fire department what to expect.

Sheriff Moses looked up at the road where cars were beginning to pile up as they slowed down to watch the fire. He waved to the state trooper and continued on walking up to the road. The trooper got out of his car and came over and asked me to back my car up to the side road so it would be out of the way when the fire trucks came. It seemed to me that it took the fire trucks about fifteen minutes to reach Leon's house, and another ten to run the hose down to the lake. By then it was too late, and about all they could do was watch the house finish burning. And it did burn really hot, until the only thing that was left of the house was one wall and a big, black circle where the fire had charred the ground. Everything that could burn did, and the stove and refrigerator and things like that were just twisted pieces of black metal.

Laurel and Jess rolled up just as the fire was dying down. They stood there watching as the remaining shell of a wall fell in with a crash, and then Laurel started walking around the black circle where the house had stood. I think Laurel was in a daze from the shock, and Jess walked with her, trying to steady her with his arm around her waist.

The firemen had been busy making sure that none of the trees around the house caught fire, and the state trooper came over and started talking to Laurel. She seemed to recognize him, and he took out a notebook and started writing. After a moment, the three of them turned around and looked at me.

By this time, other police cars had arrived, and even though it was late, the hard surface road that ran past the house, or now, where the house had been, was lined with cars and people gawking. The police up on the road set up lights, and started moving people back into their cars and sending them on their way, and there was almost an accident as drivers, blinded by the police lights, slowed down to see what was going on.

I turned to look back at the fire, only to find the state trooper standing about three feet away from me, just staring at me. He looked familiar, but in the dark with lights flashing and firemen yelling at us, I didn't realize until later who he was.

He asked me if I had been the man at the fire when Mrs. Johnson pulled up, and I said I was, adding that we arrived at almost the same time. Of course, I could guess what he wanted, besides my name and where I lived, so I told him before he could ask, and he wrote it down. After those preliminaries, I said no, as far as I could tell no one was at Leon's house when I got there, and no, I didn't see a car leaving or anyone hiding in the bushes. Then he asked if I had seen anybody down at the dock, or a boat out on the water. I had to admit I had no idea, since I hadn't thought about looking down at the lake. He gave me his card with his name and number and said he might come back tomorrow and talk to me again. He tipped his hat and left, heading for Sheriff Moses, who was walking down the driveway toward us. Without looking at it I put the card in my pocket.

I looked around for Laurel and Jess, and saw them talking to Irene. Then they turned and looked at me again, and since I was getting tired of being looked at, I waved back. They smiled, and motioned for me to come over where they were standing, talking to Irene.

We stood together in a little circle, and I hugged Laurel and said how sorry I was, but before we could say anything else, there was big commotion down at the dock where a big, fancy new speedboat had pulled up and was gunning its engine in reverse as it slowed down. Since the dock light was always on, I could see a man jump out and tie up the boat. He looked up at the house and came walking toward us, and was followed by a pretty woman wearing a baseball cap. They were both wearing blue shirts and white Bermuda shorts and looked like they were just coming from a tennis match. As they got closer, the woman looked at us, and gave a wild wave of what seemed surprise. I was even more surprised, and before I could stop myself, I blurted out "Jeeesus, it's Marty."

Laurel's eyes widened, and she turned to Jess with a questioning expression. Jess just shook his head and said, "Yeah, that's right. His ex."

Marty and the man I was guessing correctly was Spiros, her new husband, stopped in front of us, and there was an embarrassed pause as I introduced my ex-wife and her new husband. The state trooper, who must have been watching, came up and began asking Marty and her husband how long they had been out on the lake. The man said they saw what looked like fire starting up, and that they were in a house across the lake, and they thought they would come over and see if they could help, and find out what was going on.

The trooper asked if they had seen a boat coming from this side of the lake, and Marty said that it was dark, but that they thought they did see something that could have been a boat moving down the lake away from the direction of the fire, but, as she said, it was dark and the distance was too great.

Standing there listening, I realized that this was the same trooper that had been standing on the porch at Leon's house, and who was also in the photograph I found in the desk drawer, the trooper standing impassively on one side of the platform as Mother and Sarah Ebersole, Joyce and Irene's mother, stood watching.

After a moment, the trooper turned and walked back toward the road. I thought that maybe it was time to leave and said goodnight, thinking that this might elicit some kind of explanation from Marty, since I was sure that their arrival was no accident, but she said nothing, and so I turned around and headed for my car. I learned later, no surprise here, that I wasn't the one they had travelled three thousand miles to see. It was the news of Leon's death that made them jump on Spiros's private jet. My being from North and knowing Leon was interesting, in a coincidental sort of way, but Laurel was the important one. I would start putting all of this together later that night as I tried to go to sleep, but right then, as I left the charred ruins of Leon's house, I knew where I was going and that I had better hurry.

Because of the big traffic jam in front of Leon's house, it took me about twenty minutes to reach Irene Ebersoles, even though it was just a few hundred yards away. When I finally did get there, a dog was sitting on the porch looking at me in a reproachful way, as if I were the one that made her miss all the excitement. Irene must have been caught in the traffic, too, and I gave her a little wave as she drove up, where I was standing on the porch waiting.

Irene opened the door and let her dog in, then turned to me and said, "I thought that you would be here."

We went inside and I watched as Irene filled up her dog's water dish and put a dog biscuit beside it, to make up for not taking her to the fire, she said. I waited as she went around the house checking the stove and all the lights.

Irene came back and gave me a quiet, thoughtful look. "I guess if I asked you to leave, you would say no."

I nodded and told her that we needed to talk and that now was the best time. She didn't say anything else, and I pulled out a chair at the kitchen table, but didn't sit down. I had known in advance that Irene would wait, saying nothing, and making me take the lead. Irene and her mother Sarah had seen Jess and me grow up together, and had served us many dishes of ice cream after we had fished off her dock all afternoon.

I guessed that late at night, with smoke drifting over from Leon's house, was probably as good a time as any to have our talk, and besides, I had already made one visit, and found no one at home. I was so nervous I couldn't get my mind around what to say about my mother and Leon and Nancy Ebersole Tuttle.

Irene heated up some milk and put just enough of the breakfast coffee in it to turn it brown, and we sat down at the kitchen table. I took a sip of coffee and tried to think of where to start. I decided to come at things sideways, and asked her what she thought about my ex-wife and her husband showing up out of the blue.

It was a dumb thing to say, and since Irene had never met Marty she just shrugged, and said, "Not much." Instead, she felt that Jess and Laurel had handled things pretty well, given the fact that there was still smoke coming off the charred ground where Leon's house had been.

There was a pause. "Why do you think Marty and her new husband were there?" she asked.

Seeing as how I didn't know, I tried to give Irene the most truthful answer I could.

"I think that Marty's husband Spiros must have had some kind of business arrangement with Leon, probably about real estate, and that he came to Florida to meet with some lawyers after he heard that Leon had died. Don't you think that their showing up like this, out in the middle of nowhere in north Florida, has to be more than just wildly improbable?"

Irene seemed to agree, and said, "So? What do you make of it?"

I could feel myself getting in deeper and deeper as my mind raced through all the possibilities. I wasn't sure if Irene realized that my real reason for being there, so late at night, was to find out if she and her sister Joyce, the nurse for Leon, thought that I might suspect that they, the three Ebersole women, had killed Leon, and then set fire to his house to avenge their dead sister, and that maybe my own mother, might also have been involved. Or, had I stopped by to find out if she thought Laurel and Jess might have started the fire to hide some of Leon's under-the-table business deals, or if they wanted to collect a big insurance payout for the house, or both. Or, did I think that maybe one of the several hundred people in Florida who had a reason to hate Leon might have set the fire?

"Let's just say that Spiros knew where Leon lived," I continued, "and that he had come to talk business with Laurel, as Leon's only heir. What was improbable to me was that they showed up on the very night Leon's house burned down, and motored across the lake seeming to pretend that they didn't know that it was Leon's house that was on fire." I looked at Irene and said, "Don't you think Marty was trying just a little too hard to look surprised when they walked up to us?"

"I did notice that," Irene said. Then she added, "How much money do you think this is about?"

"A lot. Marty's husband is probably a billionaire, or something close to it. You don't have that kind of money and not know how to take care of it."

"So there we all were," Irene said, trying to get her head around it. "Marty and her new husband, her ex-husband, me, Jess, and Jess's girlfriend Laurel, who just happens to be Leon's daughter, whose father, Leon, was in a business deal with Marty's new husband, all standing there as they watch the smoke rise from Leon's home in the middle of the night."

"These are not just coincidences, are they?" I asked.

"So what did I leave out?" Irene looked straight back at me.

I looked away, and then thought, why not say it? I took a deep breath.

"That maybe you and Joyce, and your mother killed Leon," I said. "And that my mother was involved until she died. You all grew up together and you all had a motive to kill Leon. The Ebersoles for what he did to Nancy and my mother for Leon's calling in the debt on our orange groves as soon as my father died. You were Leon's nearest neighbor, and Joyce was his nurse. You were supposed to be looking out for Leon when Laurel wasn't around."

"It's possible," Irene said softly. "And there was someone else."

"Who was that, Irene? Was it somebody I know?"

Irene paused. "No, I don't think you knew him."

"Who was it?"

Irene's voice dropped to a whisper. "A policeman. He loved Nancy."

So here it is, I thought, looking at Irene, and thinking of the dead Nancy, the young girl we once knew. Almost clear at last. I guessed there was much more to the story than what I knew, or thought I knew, but I was just too tired to say anything more. We both stood up at same time.

I waited, not moving and expecting Irene to say something more, but she just kept looking at me with a puzzled expression, so I turned sand tarted walking away.

"Hal," Irene called just as my hand went out to open the door. I turned back. "What happened, Hal?"

"They're dead, Irene. That's all."

"No, I mean what happened to you, Hal."

I took a couple of steps back toward Irene, stunned by her question and not sure what she meant. "I'm older."

Irene shook her head. "No, it's not that. The same little boy I knew is still there, I can see it in your face. But you're not the same now. It's when you talk. When you talk you become someone else. I can't quite put my finger on it."

"Don't worry, Irene. I'm still Hal, Grace's son and Jess's brother . . ." I paused, "and Nancy's friend. I'm not here to hurt anybody."

"No, I don't believe you are, Hal." Irene paused. "It's just that . . ." Her voice trailed off.

"It's just what, Irene?"

"I wasn't there when Leon was killed, and none of the others ever talked about it. So I can't say what happened. We didn't really want him dead long as he was sending Nancy the money."

"But Nancy died and Leon had a stroke."

"Yes."

"So wasn't that enough. Why kill him?"

Irene shook her head in wonderment, as if it were something she had never considered.

"I'm not really sure we did kill him." Irene looked at me for a moment and then added, "Your mother wanted us to, but she got sick and then died and we stopped talking about it." Irene reached out and grabbed the arm of a chair to steady herself. "It was all so strange."

The night air was cool on the porch. As I walked away, I could hear the door close behind me, leaving me with a vision of the people I loved, and imagining my mother with her fierce anger, acting swiftly as she brought the blow down on Leon's head.

THIRTEEN

Café Express

My mind was still reeling from the fire, even two days later. Seeing my ex-wife with her new billionaire husband dock their speedboat in front of Leon's burning house was almost as great a shock as watching Leon assault Nancy Ebersole twenty years earlier on the same spot. I needed to focus on something, but I wasn't sure what. I watched Jess and Laurel give each other relieved looks as I left and headed back toward our old home, where I still had a lot of work to do, sorting out what to keep and what to throw away. I suddenly felt that I needed to go somewhere else, where I could calm down and focus on what had been happening, but in my old-North mind, I couldn't think where that would be, since the North imprinted on my childhood memory was the North of twenty years ago, and that North didn't even have a small Minute Mart where I could buy a pre-made sandwich. But that was the old North. As I hit the first gas station at the junction of the main highway and the lake road, I saw a neon light and a sign that said "Café Express," and I remembered noticing it the first day I came home. It was open, with three cars parked in front. I went inside, feeling as if I were suddenly in another country, which, in a way, was true.

Café Express was all hillbilly chic inside, with guitar twanging music, wooden tables with red and white checkered tablecloths, glossy new stained plank siding for the walls, and big beams across the ceiling. Deer heads with glassy eyes and bass heads with mouths wide open were mounted everywhere, and the menu featured fried fish baskets, burgers, fries, onion rings and cold beer. A Confederate flag was stretched across the back wall with a hallway that led to the restrooms. Amazingly, for North, a salad bar was in the middle of the room. The bartender was giving me a friendly look and I guessed that after nine he was also taking orders from the menu, so I waved hello and said "How about a cheeseburger with fries and a cold Coors Lite." The bartender smiled and reached for a bottle, popped the top and put a glass beside it, then disappeared into the kitchen to start my burger and fries. I walked over and poured my beer, and stood watching as the head foamed up nicely.

I sat down with my back to the wall so I could look around. Two couples were at tables on opposite sides of the room, their heads down and leaning toward each other, talking in an intimate, late night way. A woman was seated in one of the booths that ran along the large front windows. Her back was to me, and I could see there was an open briefcase on the table with some papers that were spread out in front of her. She seemed to be writing something on a yellow tablet. I watched her for a moment, trying to place her in some kind of recognizable social slot, and I thought maybe a young lawyer working late, but I couldn't seem to make the right fit. Somehow, she looked familiar, and then, unexpectedly, she stopped writing and turned and looked at me in a steady, unflinching way, and there she was. It was Claire. I stared back and after a moment Claire gave the faintest ironic flicker of a smile. I pushed my chair back and stood halfway up, and then sat back down because my legs seemed to belong to someone else. After another try I managed to stand up and, beer in hand, wobble in a wavy line over to Claire's booth.

We did nothing but look at each other for a long, long time. I reached out to take her hand. She pulled hers away, picked up my beer and took several large swallows, wiped off some of the foam from her mouth and then smiled.

Before we could take this any further, the bartender arrived with my order. He put the platter down in front of me and winked at Claire. "Well, I see you two must be old friends."

Claire pulled my burger and fries over in front of her. "Never seen him before," she said. Then she took a big bite of my burger, and chased it with another long swallow of my Coors Lite.

I pointed to the platter and said "I'll have what she's having."

The bartender gave me a grin. "I love it when couples find each other," he said, before disappearing back into the kitchen.

Claire poured some ketchup on her plate.

I opened with a lame, "Been here long?"

"Long enough to want to leave."

"You should have grown up here."

Claire shrugged. "But I didn't. This is my first time."

I waited, then I asked a real question. "Why didn't you call me and say you were coming."

"I wasn't sure."

Claire was desirable as hell, sitting across from me late at night in a beer joint, with her loose hair tumbling around her shoulders. Then I looked closer and saw how tired she looked, and I remembered her last encounter with her editor, Roger, at the paper she worked for. "Did something happen with Roger?"

Claire nodded. "It sure did."

"And?"…

I could see Claire's hand start to tremble as she picked up my glass for another swallow of beer.

"He said I could come down here and write a big story about the life and brutal murder of Leon Putnam, or I could quit."

"How long have you been here?"

Claire took a deep breath. "As they say out west, I just pulled into town."

Claire's shoulders began to sag, and she looked out the window. I guessed she must have driven straight through from Boston. "Did you get any sleep?"

"A couple of hours at a rest stop."

"I couldn't believe it when I saw you get out of the car. You walked right by the window. What made you come here?"

I tried to hide my smile. "Well, I wasn't looking for you."

"Are you glad to see me?"

Before I could answer, the bartender came up with my order. He put it down and disappeared without any more wiseass remarks.

I took her hand. "I'm staying at the house where I grew up. Jess asked me to take care of it after mother's funeral. I'm the only one there. I want you to stay with me."

Claire squeezed my hand. "I'm not sure. It would be complicated, don't you think, with all you have going on?"

"No. I've been away so long that the people here don't even know who I am. I'm just glad you're here.

Claire hesitated. I knew what she was thinking. That she was here to talk to people and ask a lot of questions, and that what she had to find out would involve my family, and if it became personal, it might stop her from doing her job.

"Don't worry," I added. "I can fill you in on what I know and what I don't know, and tell you about who the people are, but I want you to stay with me tonight." I paused and just looked at her for a moment. "I almost fell over when I saw you turn around."

There was flicker of a smile from Claire. "Yeah, I could tell."

We finished eating and I settled the tab, then I walked with Claire to her car. "Just follow me. You can park your car behind our house."

Claire gave me a quizzical look.

"Jess might come over early," I explained. "We should talk before you start interviewing the usual suspects."

We went past Butt's grocery store, now abandoned, with the roof falling in. It had been an old house which the Butts had converted into a store, with some small rooms in the back where they lived. Our driveway was about fifty yards past the store. I slowed down and turned in, crossed the now useless cattle guard and circled around to the back of the house. Claire pulled in beside me and got out.

"You're sure this is okay?"

"I'm sure."

Claire looked around. It was dark, and in the moon-light, the Spanish moss looked like old familiar ghosts hanging in the live oaks. About fifty yards away we could see Lake Rosa shining through the trees like a plate of molten silver.

"This is amazing," Claire said. "How many lakes are there around here?

"There are hundreds of spring-fed lakes in this part of the state. The water in our lake is so pure we still drink from it."

"What is it called?"

"Lake Rosa. It's pretty small, about two miles across. That was Swan Lake behind Butts's Store. It's two or three times as large as our lake, and back in town, Lake Santa Fe is huge."

Claire ran ahead a few yards so she could see the lake. She looked back at me as I walked toward her. I could see how she loved the lake and the Florida landscape in the moonlight. But I could feel my own response to her being here with me at this moment, with death and murder and the memories from growing up in North wrapped around me like a tangled net, and I was shocked to feel that I wished she had not come, bringing an assignment to find out as much as possible about Leon's murder, something so close to my family and friends, something that I would not name and that I didn't really want her to know, and I realized how the very place was part me, and that my feelings and the house I grew up in, and North itself, were part of something larger, with fibers intertwined around things receding behind me deep into the past, things that she might never understand.

"Are you okay, Hal?"

Claire's voice jolted me back into the present and I found myself standing next to her, with her hands reaching out toward me. "You seemed so far away."

"Do you want to know the truth?"

Claire paused for a moment, then smiled. "Of course. I'm a reporter, remember."

"Then don't be upset. I'll explain later. It's just that I realized that it's you being here that isn't okay."

Claire flinched, and moved back away from me, her face almost invisible now in the darkness. I waited.

"You're sorry I came?"

"It's hard to explain. I love you, but not here in North."

"I promise, I won't get in the way."

"You already have. Jess might drop by in the morning, and maybe Laurel."

"I can take a room at a motel. If you want to be with me, you can come there. Or, we can meet in another town." She reached in a pocket and held up her phone. "We both have these."

Claire paused, and then moved closer. "Tell me, what is it that you're afraid of?"

"As you said, you're a reporter, and that means you have to find out facts about Leon, Laurel's father, and then write a story. A story about North and who killed Leon Putnam and why. When you give it to your editor, it has to make sense. It has to be complete. But I'm beginning to find out my own story, and I don't think it can ever be clearly told."

"Why not?"

"Because I can never find out what truth is. Too much time has passed, and I can only guess at what happened."

"It can still be just your story, Hal. Whatever I find out and whatever I write will be my story, just what I uncover, and what other people tell me. What's wrong with that?"

I couldn't answer. I was baffled by my own feelings and her sense that we had nothing to worry about. What the hell, I thought. Maybe we don't have anything to worry about.

I could feel my body relax, and I gave up trying to make sense of it all.

That night we made love and then we took a vow together that tomorrow I would continue clearing out mother's house, and that Claire would find a motel where she could work alone and write her story about Leon Putnam. Finally, we both agreed, we would spend the nights together.

We were up early, and over coffee I suggested that Claire should begin by doing research online, maybe at the University in Gainesville. Then she could start with some interviews. I would give her some names and background information.

Claire paused. "Can I use you as a reference?"

I thought this over, and then smiled. "Sure, though it won't do you much good. I've been away too long. You'll have to explain who I am to most people."

We agreed that I would not read what Claire ended up writing. This would be Claire's story. In the meantime, I would go on packing all the family stuff I had started to put in some kind of order.

I walked Claire out to her car and watched as she drove away. As I turned toward the house, for some reason I thought about the photograph of Leon's award ceremony in Palatka, and once inside I began searching for it. I was positive that I had left the photograph on the desk where I had been working, buried under a stack of other papers. Now, after searching through all the papers on the desk, and then going through the desk drawers and the cardboard boxes stacked up on the floor, filled with everything from old bank accounts to my mother's recipes and cookbooks, I had to admit that the photograph was missing.

Maybe memory is like the stacks of old magazines and papers I have already boxed and sent to the dump, stacks of papers that seemed, to us, so important as we carefully filed them away.

After a couple of hours searching for the photograph I gave up, and for the rest of the day I pushed myself to finish the job of packing, not eating until supper and then falling in bed, exhausted and drained of all feelings.

I could feel sleep coming on, and I understood somehow that I was entering a world where I was always running, pursued by relentless shadows that followed my every move. I passed a burning house. A woman stood on the porch, frantically yelling "Save yourself!" She disappears. I come to a river. Someone on the other bank cries out "Get in the boat!" I am floating down the river. Water splashes around me. Helpless, I begin sinking down into the river's green darkness. I let go of my life.

For a long time there was nothing, and then I woke up, with the morning sun shining in my eyes. Frantically looking around, I realized that I was in North, in the house where I grew up.

For some reason I think of a line from Yeats: *And therefore I have sailed the seas and come/To the holy city of Byzantium.* And here I am in North, with my parents' belongings spread out around me on various chairs and tables, or filed away in the empty boxes I found at the local dump, and that now fill the room, and unable to remember where, only yesterday, I had placed a photograph. Home, I thought, will always have something sacred about it, no matter where it is.

I tried to connect a few things from the day before in the hope that it would jog loose something in my memory, but nothing came. It had been a long day that ended with the fire at Leon's, a visit with Jess and Laurel at Laurel's place, then meeting Claire at the diner. And now, here I was in the house I grew up in, wondering who would want to steal an old photograph of Leon Putnam receiving an award at a park in Palatka? Nobody, as far as I could tell. And yet, my mother and Nancy Ebersole's mother were in the crowd, there at the ceremony, and my mother had saved the photograph. Why?

I walked over to the large window in the study and stood by the chair where my father liked to sit. A box for flowers had been put on the outside sill, supported by some metal brackets, and filled with the pink geraniums my mother tended. A white butterfly floated by, the one with our state's name, a Florida White. Maybe that was a good sign. I continued my sorting and packing, not believing for a moment that I would find something that would answer my questions about the missing photograph.

The work was tedious, and after filling two boxes I went back to the kitchen to prepare my usual breakfast of coffee and two pieces of buttered toast. When I finished, I washed the dishes and then started putting things away before I wiped off the table. I poured my last cup of coffee and sat down, not thinking of anything really. That was when I noticed I had missed a napkin, which had been neatly folded and placed between the salt and pepper shakers. I reached over and as I picked the napkin up, the photograph fell out and fluttered lightly down on the table, landing with the picture side showing, so I could see the crowd and Leon, with the impassive state trooper standing behind him, still looking straight ahead.

I sat down to finish my coffee and pull together my scattered feelings. I was relieved when I remembered that I was the one who had moved the photograph to the kitchen. "I did it all myself," Sophocles has Oedipus say. It was comforting to know that.

FOURTEEN

Sheriff Moses

I had been working for an hour packing thirty-year old *National Geographic* magazines into a large cardboard box, and then, when I tried to lift it, I realized my mistake and started repacking them into smaller boxes. I had asked the man at the town dump to put aside good boxes for me, and made a note to go by and pick up some more.

The town dump was one luxury that had been added since I left home, and I thought about my childhood, and how we disposed of our garbage when I was growing up. Our soil was loose and sandy, which made for easy digging, and everyone had a garbage pit behind the house where they dumped the garbage. Once a week my dad would go find the kerosene can and pour the kerosene over the garbage and then set it on fire. If you dug it deep enough, a good garbage pit would last about six months before you had to fill it back in and dig another one.

I finished the *National Geographic*s and started carrying the boxes out to the old pickup my mother maintained. As I brought out the last box, Sheriff Moses was there, leaning against his car. When I was growing up, Sheriff Moses was famous for putting up an election poster on the window of North's one gas station which told about how he would maintain law and order, was always fair, and had a great conviction rate, and that he would appreciate our vote on his behalf. Then, at the bottom of the poster, he had handwritten, "If anyone has information about who stole my lawnmower, please contact me." Then, he signed it across the bottom of the poster. For years, people asked him if he had got his lawnmower back yet.

"Hello, Sheriff, what's up?" I said, not being really sure about why he was there.

"I just needed to ask you a few questions."

Without thinking, I said, "No problem, although I don't know how much help I can be."

Sheriff Moses gave me a puzzled look. "Why do you say that?"

"Well, I left North ten years ago, and I didn't come home until after Leon was murdered. So, all I really know is just what the papers are saying."

Sheriff Moses cocked his head sideways and said, "Hal, this isn't about Leon's murder. It's about the fire."

"Oh," I said.

"What makes you think I wanted to talk to you about Leon's murder?"

I could feel my throat tighten. "Well, I don't know. I guess you thought I might have heard something."

Sheriff Moses slowly considered this, and then changed direction. "Irene Johnson says that you were the first on the scene at the fire."

"You know, I'm not so sure about that. I thought Irene was there when I drove up."

There was a moment's pause as he took out a small notebook and read a couple of pages.

"No, she was certain you were there when she drove up. I just talked to her about it." He tapped his notebook with his pen for emphasis.

"I think I told you at the fire that I thought Irene was there first, but I couldn't be sure about it. Besides, if I was there first, she drove up right after me. Does it really matter?"

"It all depends. The first person there might have seen something that nobody else did."

I shook my head. "The house was already burning pretty good when I drove up. I could see the flames from the road. That's what made me stop."

"I can understand that. But then again, if the fire was burning so you could see it from the road, why didn't somebody else stop. Was your car the only one on the road?"

"I can't remember. It was really late. I was just driving around trying to clear my head and see what was new in my old hometown." There was a pause. "What about Jess and Laurel?" I asked. "Have you talked with them?"

"Yes, but both you and Irene confirm that they came later."

I couldn't think of anything else to say. Sheriff Moses closed his notebook.

"Think about it, and if anything else comes to mind let me know. I may have to call you in to make an official statement."

"Sure, no problem." I could feel myself relax. Sheriff

Moses took a step away, and then turned back.

"By the way, Hal. There's a young woman in town who's a reporter. She says she's writing a story about Leon's murder for a paper in Boston. She claims you know her."

"Uh. . . .Yes, that's right. We're good friends."

Sheriff Moses paused and then looked at the ground, and kicked some sand with his boot.

"I'm glad to hear that. I'll be going on. Oh, and stay here in town for the next week or so. As I said, I may need you to make a statement."

There was a click of recognition in my head. I looked at the sheriff and smiled. "I can do that. I think the last statement I made in your office was when you caught me with Jimmie Spitz racing on that back road near Lake Serena."

Sheriff Moses smiled, and I could tell that he remembered.

"Well, this is a little different." He paused, and said "I guess you know Jimmie's out on parole?"

"Out. You mean?" My voice trailed off.

"You've been away a long time, Hal. Jimmie was serving five years for possession."

All I could think of was the Jimmie Spitz I knew, who always sat behind me in our ninth grade geometry class so he could copy my paper. I truly didn't know what to say.

"It's all drugs now, Hal. We're still remote from Miami and all the rich people. There are still places to get lost in, and start making meth. All I do now is hide out in the swamps and wait for the action to start."

"What about good old-fashioned murder?"

"You mean Leon?"

To my surprise, Sheriff Moses stepped closer, almost crowding me back, and lowered his voice. "A lot of people think that Leon was part of it. He was the go-to person in

Tallahassee. Anything around here that got done, legal or otherwise, he knew about. He had to have a lot of enemies. If you know anything, you need to tell me now."

"No," I said, "all of this is news to me. After ten years, I'm really out of touch." Sheriff Moses gave me a long look.

"So why did you immediately ask about Leon and drugs?"

I shrugged. "Well, you know better than anybody, Sheriff. You know my family has a history with Leon."

"I hope that's what it is."

Sheriff Moses gave me one final stare, and said, "I'll call you about that statement," and then turned away.

"Glad to help, Sheriff, anytime." I gave him a fake smile, while feeling my stomach turn over, and thinking that this man is convinced I'm lying. Just at that moment Claire's car came down the driveway and rolled to a stop beside the sheriff. Claire jumped out and waved at him.

"Hi, Sheriff Moses. What are you doing here?"

Now it was the sheriff's turn to look uncomfortable.

"Oh, nothing much, young lady. Nothing much at all. Just catching up on old times."

We watched as the Sheriff gunned his engine, backed up and then roared away, tires spinning dirt over my mother's flower beds.

Claire came over and gave me a hug.

"What was that all about?"

"It wasn't about what I thought it was going to be about."

She could see I was upset. "Did I do something wrong?"

"No."

"What about you? Are you in trouble?"

I waited before answering. I wanted to say just the

right thing and not let my anger at myself spill over.

"No, I don't think so. Let's go inside and talk."

"Great. I brought us some lunch from Café Express, our favorite restaurant, aka 'Our Place.' Oh, and by the way, Eddie sends you his best."

"And Eddie is?"

Claire went over to her car and came back with a big brown paper bag that I could tell had been carefully packed.

"Eddie is my new best friend, and our favorite bartender."

I couldn't help but smile as she pulled me toward the house.

Without thinking, I steered her toward the front of the house. I could feel Claire's hand pulling toward the side door, which was closer.

"This way," I said, pointing toward the front of the house.

Claire gave me a funny look as she walked behind me. "The side door is closer."

All I could think of to say was, "We never used the side door."

Claire gave me a funny look, and just said, "Oh," but not the 'oh' that means okay, but the one that means tell me more.

"The side door leads directly into the kitchen."

"But that's where we're going."

"Yes, that's where we're going," I replied.

We went in by the front door, through the living room and into the kitchen. Claire unpacked her bag of burgers and two small salads, while I got out some paper plates and plastic cups. She had filled the bag with little packets of salt and pepper, mustard, mayonnaise, and bigger packets of salad dressing. She dumped them out on the table and sat down.

Claire pointed to the scattered packets of condiments. "I was sure there wouldn't be any of these around, so I brought a few things."

"This is great. I keep meaning to buy some groceries."

We were quiet for a few moments enjoying the burgers and salads, then Claire sat back in her chair and gave me a look.

"So, why didn't you want to use the kitchen door?"

"Does it matter?"

Claire flushed a little, but didn't back off. "No, not to me, but I sensed that it did matter to you, and I wondered why."

"We did use the kitchen door sometimes, if Mom wanted us to take out the trash, or go pick some oranges. But she didn't want people coming directly from outside into her kitchen, especially company. So we used the front door."

I paused, thinking of the thousands of times I had followed that rule as a boy and turned away and walked toward the front of the house.

I looked at Claire. "When you started walking toward the kitchen door, it was like I could feel my mother's presence, and she would be there, waiting to say, "Go around to the front, Hal. And wipe your feet before you come in.""

Claire looked at me, and for some reason we both started to laugh.

After a moment, Claire picked up a few packets of salt and held them up. "Maybe that's why you haven't bought any groceries?"

I could only nod my head and say, "That's probably true. Also, I kept putting it off, thinking I would be leaving in a couple of days, but the Sheriff wants me to stay in town, in case I have to make a statement about the fire."

Claire shrugged and said, "Well, that won't take long."

Then she cocked her head and gave me a quizzical look, "Will it?"

I paused, not sure what to say. "There seems to be a problem about who was first on the scene at the fire. Irene Johnson's house is the next house on the lake past Leon's."

"How far away is that?"

"Oh, maybe about a quarter of a mile if you are out on the blacktop, but there is a small dirt road that runs between them and is a little closer to Leon's."

"Where were you?"

"I was out on the blacktop, on the way home. That's where I saw the fire. I turned in and drove down to Leon's house, but it was already too late. I'm sure that Irene was already there, and Irene says I was there when she drove up."

Claire paused, taking it in. "So, you both got there at about the same time?"

"Well, yes and no. Sheriff Moses wants to clear it up, since the first person at the fire could have been there for an hour or for a couple of minutes."

"Did he accuse you of anything?"

"No, not yet, anyway."

FIFTEEN

Stuff

Claire left after breakfast the next morning, still reeling from my long summary last night about the multiple relationships involving almost my entire 'North universe,' with various motives and fears about who might want to do what to whom, and my meandering tour through all the ins and outs of my life in North, and ending with what I knew or suspected about Leon's murder. Claire had finally rolled back her eyes and asked me to stop. She hesitated for a moment and then said, "This might make a good story if you ever get to the bottom of it, but to paraphrase someone whose name I can't remember, 'Who cares who killed Leon Putnam?' Or, to put it another way, why do you care?"

I couldn't blame Claire, since much of what I told her

was pure speculation. And yet . . . and yet I didn't feel that way. I still believed that my mother and the Ebersoles killed Leon, or had someone kill Leon for them, and that I needed to find out for sure what the truth was about Leon's death. It didn't matter to me if my mother and the Ebersoles were really involved. As someone said about Leon at his funeral in a loud whisper, after saying goodbye to Laurel and following the crowd flowing back to the parking area at the side of the house, "He needed killing."

All this was running through my mind as I kept packing, touching things I hadn't seen in years—old shoes, discarded address books, my mother's china and silver—and emptying out drawers filled with match covers, string and the packs of cough drops my mother would keep and could never find as she rushed out of the house late for church as usual, the loose change of life that we always mean to throw away but never do. I couldn't use any of this to explain to Claire why all of these unimportant remainders of my mother's life made me feel that everything in our house was crying out to be justified in some way, and needed to be given some kind of meaning before finally ending up at the county dump.

Like Claire, who felt the need to go back to her motel room and write about all the events surrounding Leon's murder, I went to the kitchen and started making an inventory of all the important items in our house that I thought were worth keeping, or to sell at an auction, something concrete that I could show Jess and that we could agree on.

The only thing of any real value I could find was in my mother's bedroom, where she had placed her diamond ring and necklace in a small jewelry box on her chest of drawers. I doubted that Jess would want them for Laurel. All of Mother's clothes could go to Goodwill.

I looked around to find an envelope for the ring and

necklace. I lifted up the top shelf of the jewelry box to take it downstairs, when I saw a small folded-up piece of paper. I took the paper out, carefully unfolding it, only to see three lines of numbers and letters that seemed to make no sense. They were written in my mother's hand and seemed to be in some kind of code that I could not understand. The letters and numbers were arranged in groups across the page with no explanation of their meaning. I went downstairs and dropped the jewelry and the small piece of paper in an envelope, sealed it up and wrote "jewelry box" on the outside with a list of the items I had not thrown away.

The furniture was worn out and most of it I could remember from my childhood. In the kitchen, there was an old stove, an old refrigerator and a sink with black spots where the porcelain had worn away. A small portable radio was on the kitchen counter, but no TV set anywhere in the house. The few orange trees out back, where Jess and I had thrown rotten oranges at each other, had not been tended to in years and were either dead or dying. My mother's Crown Victoria Ford was probably twenty years old or older, but still running. My father's fishing tackle box, painted over in white aluminum, with the handle wrapped in black tape, was on the garage floor next to some rakes and shovels.

I added these things to my list and looked at it for a long time, thinking how each item was like a dead person , and that they were already nothing more than words on a piece of paper, and like us they needed a quick internment.

And then, of course, there was the guilt: guilt that all of the material things in the house, and even the house itself, meant nothing to me anymore, and how, in a sense, Jess and I were like the other items in the house that I had recorded, and that we were not part of that former life anymore, and that all of the care my parents had given to building a home, and the pride they had felt having put it all together and maintaining it, was vanishing, and that its disappearance would take a part of Jess and me with it.

I worked for another hour, moving from room to room, naming each object that might have some value. Then back in the kitchen, I placed my notepad on the table. It was almost time for lunch, and I thought "Why linger?" Outside, a gentle breeze had freshened the air, and as I drove away, the trance-like oppression I felt from being inside our house slowly dissolved, leaving me with a clear mind that could think clearly about alternative possibilities for getting through the next few days.

I entered the Café Express (where else?) with my eyes on the floor, not wanting to find a gaze that might be looking back at me with recognition. Eddie, the slyly chatty waiter came up with a menu.

"Dining alone today?"

"It looks that way."

Eddie put two menus on the table. "Just in case," Eddie said, giving me his patented leering smile.

Without looking at the menu, I ordered a barbecue platter and a diet Mountain Dew.

"Good choice," Eddie said, as he left with one menu, leaving the other menu on the table, which silently implied that maybe, if I was lucky, Claire might show up. And then again, maybe she wouldn't. In about two minutes, my frosty can of Mountain Dew was on the table, sitting next to a glass filled with ice. I smiled, feeling at home. Somewhere around the South Carolina line, you stopped having to ask for a full glass of ice to go with your drink. It was just expected.

The barbecue came with two cups of sauce, the sweet Kansas City kind, and the vinegar and pepper North Carolina variety. I pushed the sweet sauce away and poured out the

North Carolina hot sauce over my barbecue and French fries. Eddie walked by, glanced at my plate and gave me a slight nod of approval. I leaned back, enjoying the aroma, then slowly took a few forkfuls and spread it out over my bun, added some cole slaw and started eating.

I took my time, enjoying the barbecue as I tried to sort out all the pieces of the puzzle I had encountered by doing nothing more than listening to what other people had to say, and trying to interpret it through the out-of-date lens of my childhood. Was the past really the key to what was happening now in the new North I didn't really know? I began to feel like a detective on a TV show, the one where there are too many suspects.

Without any warning, there was a huge crash from the kitchen, as if every dish and pot had been dropped at the same time. I heard Eddie yelling, and a tall, thin man with an apron in his hand walked out through the swinging doors, then he turned and threw the apron back toward the kitch-en. The man was rail thin, and he slowly ambled around the counter and looked around the dining room with a delighted smile, as if saying "How do you like that for a bust-up!" Then he saw me and started smiling. It was my old high school mis-fit buddy, Jimmie Spitz, who, I had just learned from Sheriff Moses, was now out of jail and back in North.

Jimmie walked toward me, tilted sideways as he walked, with long, loping steps. He gave me a crooked smile and slid into the booth, sitting across from me as he began laughing.

"I heard you were back and were out starting fires."

I didn't laugh. "Who said that? Sheriff Moses?"

"Let's just say lots of people are talking," Jimmie said, raising his eyebrows with a look that invited me to guess.

I didn't want to play that game, saying "So how long

have you been out of jail?"

Jimmie leaned back and gave me a long, hard stare. "About three months."

I didn't back off and said, "Are you staying clean?"

"I didn't go to jail for using. I was dealing."

I thought this over for a moment. "That's a big-time conviction. What happened?"

"Leon intervened on my behalf."

"So, Leon . . ." I stopped, not sure how to finish what I was trying to say.

Jimmie relaxed and, as if explaining the obvious to a child, said, "Things have changed, Hal. This isn't the North we grew up in. Drugs are everywhere and almost everybody is involved. Tell me what you want and I can have it here in ten minutes."

My mind was still racing about what Jimmie had implied about Leon, and I didn't want to let it go. "Are you saying that Leon was involved in drugs?"

"Hal, even when we were growing up, Leon was involved in everything that was going down. What do you think?"

I started fumbling for an answer. "Okay, so Leon was into drugs. But he was basically a mindless old man at the end. Why would—whoever it was—bother to kill him?"

"Why don't you ask your brother Jess that question?"

I looked at Jimmie for a moment, not sure what he meant, and then it gradually dawned on me that I had just heard something that I didn't really want to hear. I should have known all along that my thinking about North had to be out of date. But I didn't think that this new drug culture could possibly involve people I knew. Jimmie meant that Leon was part of my family, and that through Jess I was also part of Leon's family since Laurel would soon be my sister-in-law. "So, what you're saying is Laurel and Jess are part of Leon's drug enterprises?"

There was a flash of light and it seemed as if I were watching a movie unrolling in front of me, and I was back at the fire as Leon's house slowly transformed itself into a mass of glowing embers in the Florida night. I could see Sarah Ebersole as she came toward me and I began thinking, just as Sheriff Moses had asked, "Was she there first or was it you?" —and as always I realized that everything that was happening revolved around Leon and that Leon and the Ebersoles and my mother with Jess and Laurel seemed to be floating in the air like the ashes floating skyward above Leon's burning house.

Somehow my eyes came back into focus and I found myself listening as Jimmie leaned forward, and said "What I'm saying is that almost everybody in North is involved one way or the other. Some people are users and some people are dealers and some are both, but almost everybody is involved in some way."

"What makes you think that Jess and Laurel are involved in all of this?"

Jimmie gave a derisive snort. "She's Leon's daughter. Hasn't Jess moved in with her? Aren't they living together in her house, right next to Leon's? And who started the fire, anyway?"

"I was at that fire," I said. "Sarah Ebersole and I arrived at just about the same time. The house was already burning. Nobody knows who started it." I could hear how lame my words sounded.

Jimmie just shook his head. "Come on, Hal. There was something in that house no one was ever supposed to know about."

I sat there, remembering Jess and Laurel saying how

they had been moving things out of Leon's house, while Jimmie just looked at me, knowing that I knew he was right.

It was lunch time, and people were finishing up and leaving. I was expecting Claire for lunch even though I had not waited for her. Two cars had just pulled up and I could see through the big front windows Claire and Sheriff Moses coming through the front door of Café Express. Jimmie saw them at the same time I did. He jumped up and headed for the door, hoping to slide by Sheriff Moses, but just as he reached for the door, Sheriff Moses' big hand grabbed him by the shoulder. Claire looked startled, but caught my eye and moved past the Sheriff, coming toward me with a look of relief on her face. I smiled at Claire while I continued watching as the Sheriff leaned over Jimmie and started whispering in his ear.

Claire gave me a look that was too bright and said "So, what's for lunch?"

"The barbecue was good," I said, just as Eddie sidled up.

Claire nodded her head. "I'll have the barbecue."

Eddie wrote this down and started to leave, but not before I asked, "Did I hear something break in the kitchen?" I smiled and gave him an innocent "What did I say?" look as he turned and glared at me. Out of the corner of my eye I could see Sheriff Moses escorting Jimmie outside.

SIXTEEN

Dinner for Six

I was standing at the top of the drop-down ladder that went up into the attic, waiting for Jess to hand me the last few boxes that we had brought over from Leon's house before the fire. I was already dressed and stood there in Laurel's cool air-conditioned house watching Jess come back from the garage with the final load.

"At least we're finished moving," Jess said. "Now we just have to find out what we moved."

"Go take a shower," I said. "I'll fix us some drinks." Laurel had already ordered a catered dinner and put out a big pitcher of sangria that was ice cold from the refrigerator. We had a couple of hours to get ready and Jess and I needed to talk about what we might expect. I brought the sangria and glasses out to the front porch. Jess and I could talk and have a drink after he finished his shower.

I thought that the best decision Jess and Laurel had made was to start moving all of Leon's records and important papers out of his house as soon as he came home from the hospital. Of course, Leon was on the board of several banks, and Laurel thought she knew about most of his business dealings, but Leon had grown up in an earlier time, and it was the extent of his private dealings with brief descriptions of promissory notes, swaps of equipment and pay for part-time temporary workers and similar items that surprised her. He had recorded the details in hand-written notebooks that were filed away in cardboard boxes that were now up in her attic.

I was just finishing my first glass of sangria when Jess came in, fresh from the shower, toweling his head and wearing shorts and a T-shirt. "I'll take one of those," he said, pointing toward my glass. We sat there quietly for a moment, sipping our drinks.

Jess sat down and began slowly turning his drink around on the glass top of the table, "That was a good day's work."

"It's not over yet," I said.

Jess picked up his drink and looked at me. "I'll bet that you and your Boston lady, what's her name . . ."

"Claire. Her name is Claire."

"Right, Claire. Anyway, I'll bet that you and Claire come into a little something from your ex, Marty, and her billionaire husband."

"I'm not holding my breath." I started to say something else but I could hear Claire and Laurel talking as they came from the kitchen.

I felt a surge of sympathy for Laurel as she and Claire walked in. Laurel was telling Claire that when she was growing up, she was seen only as Leon's daughter, and no one would ever talk to her.

"It's still that way, isn't it?" Jess said.

"I got over it."

Jess held up his empty glass of sangria and said, "Maybe this will loosen up the Kawanakas. And if that doesn't work, maybe the Remington painting of the dying cowboy—or is it an Indian?—stashed away in the back room will help."

"Why don't you prop it up in the living room so we can all see it?" Claire asked.

"No," Laurel said with a grim smile. "I want to make Spiros ask to see it."

Jess raised his eyebrows. "I doubt if he is used to asking for anything."

I looked around with a big smile. "I wish I were rich. I'd buy it in a minute."

Jess looked at Claire. "What about you?"

"No cowboys and no heads of dead animals. I love Monet's haystacks."

It was almost evening and the lake was starting to shimmer from the slanting light of the late afternoon sun.

I was trying to put it all together, and without thinking I asked, "When do the lawyers come?" For a moment, no one said anything. I could see Jess sit up with an alert look toward Laurel, but Laurel didn't seem to mind my question.

"The lawyers will be here next week, but I'm not worried. The Frederick Remington alone will bring enough to pay the lawyers."

Jess rattled the ice in his glass. "Leon should have talked to you about it."

"I know, we were going to talk, but he kept putting it off, and then he had the stroke." Laurel stood up. "Mrs. Mc-Gahee will be here in a few minutes."

I dreaded her arrival, even though she was the best cook in Florida. She had started off near Gainesville running a boarding house. She was so good that people who were not boarders started eating there. Then the University boys started going. Her slices of roast beef were so big they fell off the plate. Rumor had it that it was Leon who had backed her when she first expanded. He never ate anywhere else when he was in town. He wanted to franchise her, but she always said no.

As if on cue, we could hear a car drive up. "Here she is now," Laurel said as she headed back toward the kitchen.

The Kawanakas arrived ten minutes later and Laurel and Spiros disappeared immediately into the back room to look at the Remington. Claire headed for the kitchen and this left Jess and me to chat with Marty. It was a long thirty minutes. Marty wanted to tell us all about her new wonderful life with Spiros, especially their homes in Greece and Los Angeles. She did a good job cataloging all of my flaws, major and minor that Jess already knew from growing up with me. "Hal was difficult to live with,   `          `" she kept repeating.

"Surprise! Surprise!" I kept thinking, but I said nothing, nodding occasionally to show that I was listening, and downing two ice cold vodka martinis from the pitcher that had replaced the sangria—at Spiros's request, as Laurel put it.

"Are you okay?" Marty's question brought me to attention, and I realized that I must have been sitting there with a dazed look on my face. As I fumbled for an answer, Claire came sauntering in, looking as if there had not been a death, a murder, a fire, a divorce that we were all part of.

Claire tried to lighten the mood, laughing and pouring drinks as she said, "I've heard he can be difficult."

"Just here in North," I said. In all other places, I am a model of the genial easy-to-live with guy."

I wanted to add, for Claire's benefit, that actually, I was not as difficult as Marty claimed, but just then Spiros and Laurel came in from the back room talking animatedly as if they had known each other for years.

"Well, hello again, everybody!" Laurel said, looking at Spiros as they both took in the situation and burst out laughing. "I'm sorry we took so long. Spiros knows so much about art, and I couldn't answer most of his questions. Anyway, we had a bet that the martini pitcher would be empty before we came back from talking and looking at the Remington. I won."

Claire looked at the pitcher she was holding. "I think you're right. Not even half a martini left."

"I was just going for a refill," I said, taking the pitcher from Claire and turning toward the kitchen, but Laurel stepped in front of me, taking the pitcher from my hands.

"You stay here and hold the fort. I'm going to check on what Mrs. McGahee left us for supper, and then I can start bringing it in."

"Can I help?" Claire sang out.

"Yes. You can come with me and bring back another pitcher of martinis."

The full pitcher of martinis came back, and then Mrs. McGahee's dinner was rolled in from the kitchen on the two large serving carts Laurel had used for the reception after Leon's funeral. We finished the fruit and sherbet for dessert, and were sipping on the after dinner wine and coffee, when Spiros asked a question about the fire.

"Sheriff Moses says he hasn't made much progress in finding out how the fire at your father's house started?"

"That's true," Laurel said.

I was hoping that would be the end of the talk about the fire, and it was, but what followed was just as bad.

Spiros looked straight at me. "He also said that you and Claire had been asking a lot of questions about Leon's death."

I knew what was coming next, but I didn't think Spiros had planned for it. I leaned back and tried to relax, the way I had practiced all my life.

"That's true. You know, Spiros, I've been away for so long that I wanted to find out more about Leon's murder. This is still my home, and Laurel, Jess, and I all grew up together. And, as you probably recall, I had just arrived in California for your wedding, but I had to leave and come back here after my mother died. As for Claire, she's writing an article about North, and of course, about Leon and what happened to him has to be a big part of it."

There was a pause. I looked at Jess, and I could tell he wasn't ready to back off. "It's surprising," I continued. "I never knew Leon was interested in art. How did you two become acquainted?"

Spiros's face went dark. "Social media."

I laughed and looked around the table, as if to include us all in the joke. "Can you believe that! Finding Leon's name on a Google search about art. I would think it would have been something more like a real estate search. That's what Florida is all about. And hotels, we don't want to leave them out."

Spiros's teeth glittered as he smiled back at me. "I can handle the real estate, that's my business. And, yes, I was surprised when Leon's name came up about the Remington painting. I didn't think Leon knew much about art, but he did have a surprisingly wide range of people who knew a lot about many things."

I wasn't sure what was going to happen next. I had been watching Marty watching Claire and Spiros watching me and Laurel watching all of us, when Claire suddenly stood up.

"Well, I don't know about the rest of you, but I have an early interview in Gainesville tomorrow morning." She stopped, and gave me a "there will be no argument" kind of look.

I stood up, looked around and stretched back on my heels, then looked at Laurel. "That was a great dinner. You know, I had almost forgotten about Mrs. McGahee." I looked at Marty and Spiros and said, "When I was in junior high I used to wash dishes and serve her boarders after school. She had been a nurse and had a phobia about germs. As a boy, I was always walking around with my hands in my pockets. She kept warning me about it, worried, I guess, about what the customers might say. One day, when I wouldn't stop doing it, she pinned my pockets up."

I stood still for a moment, as the memories came flooding back and then I yelled out, "Every word of that is true." I can still see myself coming home, saying nothing, but pointing to my pockets, which were still pinned up, and grinning, as if to say, "You see, she finally did it."

Claire looked at me, delighted with my story, and said, "We'd better go before any more stories come out."

"I'm finished with the personal stories, anyway," I said. Before I could say anything else, Spiros stood up and gave Claire a hug, and I shook Spiros's hand while Claire said goodbye to Laurel.

There was the usual round of polite compliments. Marty and Spiros wanted to make an early start so they would have some time to meet with a gallery owner in Savannah and see what he had to show them. Spiros would be contacting Laurel in a few days about where to ship the Remington. They had agreed on a price and Spiros would call his office in San Francisco in the morning and have the money sent to Laurel's bank account as soon as the painting arrived.

Another round of hugs and kisses, followed by how beautiful the setting by the lake was, how the party was delightful, and reassurances from Laurel that she would write Spiros soon about whatever it was they had talked about in the back room. Then the Kawanakas made their exit. Claire and I stood there smiling as they left. From out of nowhere, a half-remembered line from high school English came floating back: "Into the night these lovers fled away."

"I begged them to stay for drinks," I heard Laurel say. "It seems like they were determined to leave."

I poured a couple more vodka martinis. We sat down and gave each other "can you believe it" looks. There was a pause. Laurel smiled, and said "$950,000. I could have gotten more if Daddy had been more careful about the provenance."

"That didn't seem to bother Spiros," I said.

"No, and neither one of us wanted to go into more details. Besides, it's Spiros's problem now. With his connections, I'm sure he can figure out something."

"So you're not worried?"

Laurel shrugged. "No, it's just a picture I inherited and then sold."

"But not every painting in the back room is worth $950,000," I added.

Claire smiled, "Caveat emptor."

SEVENTEEN

Claire Heads North

It was 10:30 as we pulled out of Laurel's driveway. I didn't realize how tense I was. I looked at Claire, thinking her face might reveal her feelings, or give me a clue that she had something to say about the evening. The waning moon gave just enough light through the trees to create shadows and I watched the alternating light and dark stripes flicker across her face as we drove, but her expression gave nothing away.

We were on the black top road that circled around the lake and after about two miles we reached the fork where you could continue west around the lake back to my old home, or you could head back east toward North. I followed the road west around the lake.

Claire either didn't want to talk or was waiting for me

to say something, so I decided to go ahead with the safest question, "So what did you think?"

Out of the corner of my eye I could see Claire lean forward, looking down at her clenched hands as if she were hoping they would open and reveal exactly the right words for what she wanted to say.

"I think that Laurel and Jess are under a lot of pressure, and that there was so much hidden history tonight that nobody wanted to talk about and probably our not talking about it was the best thing to do."

Our eyes met for just a second, and I could see her looking at me with a grim little smile of what I took to be support, while at the same time she was trying to hide something like fear, as if she was just becoming aware that it had been there all the time.

After a moment of silence she took a breath and said, "I don't think I can go on pretending too much longer that I'm just visiting you. I introduce myself as your friend and then immediately switch to asking about the murder of Leon Putnam."

"What do you think we should do about it?"

"It?" Claire shot back. "That's just it, and when people can talk about 'it' at least I'll know more about 'it' than I know now, which is nothing."

"Did tonight help?"

"Jesus! Hal," Claire exploded. "You were there. What do you think?"

"Well, sometimes nothing" . . . I paused, suddenly realizing how dumb the rest of my sentence was going to sound.

"Well," Claire queried? "Go on."

Unable to stop, I blundered ahead. "I just mean that sometimes 'nothing' can provide useful information."

"Great! It's such a comfort to know that. I'll write my editor tomorrow and tell him my article is about nothing."

Without thinking, I slowed the car down and did a U-turn and headed back where the road forked to go back to town.

"What are you doing?"

I could see Claire looking at me, puzzled and mad at the same time. "I want a grilled cheese sandwich and a cup of coffee."

Claire turned her head toward the window and said, "I give up. How can you eat anything more after that huge meal at Laurel's?"

We pulled into the Café Express and went inside. Two couples were there, sitting in the booths near the front windows. We took a booth near the counter against the side wall and waited for Eddie to come out. "On second thought," I said, "I think I'll have a beer with my sandwich. What about you?"

Claire shrugged. "Just a beer and a bag of chips."

Trying to appear calm and understanding I asked, "So what is this 'it' you were talking about?"

Claire gave me a deadeye look. "Oh, it's not hard to figure out, up to a point. A local big shot is murdered, his house is burned down, the Sheriff thinks that maybe you are involved, and all of the locals don't know anything, or, if they do know, they won't talk about it, and you think your mother was maybe involved in the murder, but you aren't sure." Claire paused, and then added, "Oh, and your old high school buddy is out of the slammer and maybe is dealing drugs again." Another pause. "So, when I talk to people, I get this sense of a vague 'it' that is out there, and that everybody but me knows what 'it' is." There was another pause, followed by another deadeye look. "And worst of all," Claire continued, "you tell me that 'it' is nothing, and that 'nothing' can really be something."

"I know," I mumbled. "I was just trying to . . ." But before I could finish, Claire hit the top of the table with her open palm with a crack so loud the other two couples turned and looked at us.

Claire leaned forward, holding her thumb and index finger so close they were almost touching, and hissed, "Dammit, Hal, stop bullshitting! I'm this close to leaving tomorrow morning, and you don't even know why."

"So tell me."

Claire looked at me, her eyes searching my face. "I'm scared. The people I talk to look at me with these angry expressions, but then say nothing. Or else they're frightened, and whisper for me to please go away and leave them alone."

Claire was right. I really had not been paying attention. But before I could say anything else, I noticed that Eddie the cook/waiter was standing beside us. We both looked up, startled. Neither one of us had seen him coming. "This looks intense," Eddie said with a pleased smile.

For once, Claire didn't play up to him. "It is," she said flatly, giving him a hard look.

Eddie's eyes widened, and his smile disappeared.

"She wants a beer and chips, and I want a beer and a grilled cheese sandwich."

"And bring me a glass of water," Claire added.

Eddie turned and headed back toward the kitchen.

Claire looked at me and almost smiled. "So are you going to talk to me?"

"I changed my mind." I started to say something lame like how I was going to do better, but out of the corner of my eye I could see headlights flash as another car pulled into the parking lot and stopped. A tall, thin man got out of the car on the driver's side while a woman in the passenger seat slid over behind the wheel. The car lights remained on with the engine running. The man walked up the steps, wavering slightly, and then pushed open the door. It was Jimmie Spitz. His clothes were wrinkled and dirty and he had that vacant eyed look of the long-time drug addict. He stopped at the counter and pulled out a gun that was stuffed in his pants. His hands were trembling, and he yelled out, "Hey, Eddie! I'm here to collect the rent."

Eddie came flying out of the kitchen as the two couples by the windows slipped out the front door. Claire had put her head down on the table and crumpled over against the wall as far as she could go.

Jimmie waved the gun and said, "Give me the black bag."

Eddie didn't seem to know what the gun meant. "You must be crazy."

Without hesitating, Jimmie fired and Eddie staggered back and fell through the kitchen door. Jimmie calmly walked behind the counter, reached down and pulled out a large, black satchel, opened it, turned it upside down and, when nothing fell out, threw it down by Eddie.

I glanced outside and saw that Sheriff Moses had pulled in behind Jimmie's car, blocking it so there was no way Jimmie could drive away. The sheriff must have been tipped off because a deputy was already dragging a handcuffed woman out of Jimmie's car, while Sheriff Moses came up the steps. What followed was like an old-fashioned Western. Sheriff Moses pushed the door open and came in with his gun drawn, and for just a moment they faced each other waiting to see who would make the first move.

Jimmie stood there, wavering back and forth, then fired a shot. Sheriff Moses fired back. Jimmie's shot blew out one of the windows. Sheriff Moses' shot hit Jimmie in the chest. The Sheriff holstered his gun and walked over and looked down at Jimmie, bleeding on the floor.

The room seemed to be slowly spinning around and I realized I was gripping the edge of the table so hard I couldn't let go. There was a low, soft sound and I looked over and saw Claire, huddled against the wall, sobbing with her hand over her mouth, and her head down on the table.

Sheriff Moses came over and gently put his hand on Claire's shoulder. "It's all over now. You're safe."

Claire grabbed his arm and he helped her out of the booth. After that, the legal routines took over. More police cars came roaring in, sirens wailing, followed by the rescue squad wagons that would carry Eddie and Jimmie away. After talking to us for a moment, Sheriff Moses let us go home telling us we must come by his office in the morning to make a statement.

As we drove back home, both of us were silent, stunned by what we had just witnessed. Claire gradually stopped shaking and then she sat up straight in her seat and said, "Well, I guess I've got something to write about now."

"So you're going to stay and finish your story?"

Claire shook her head. "The story finished back there in the café. I just need to write it up."

I didn't say anything for a moment, trying to understand what she meant. "So you're staying?"

Claire looked at me. "No, I'm leaving in the morning." There was another pause, and Claire asked, "What are you going to do?"

I was still in shock after seeing two people shot at the Café Express and I hesitated for a moment. Then suddenly, I knew what to say. "I'm going back with you."

"Are you sure?"

"Absolutely. There's nothing here for me without you."

"What about your mother's house and her estate?"

"Jess can have the house, and there's not much of an estate left. I'll call him in the morning. I can leave him a note about what I have done as far as the packing goes. He can figure it out."

By this time we had reached our driveway, and as we turned in I could see our car headlights reflecting off another car parked by our house. I tapped the brake until we were just inching forward. "We've got company."

Claire grabbed my arm. "I'm not going up there."

We waited for a few seconds, looking at the outline of the car parked in the yard. "I think we're okay," I said. "If somebody was coming after us they wouldn't leave their car in plain sight."

We slowly moved forward until we were behind the other car, but before I could do anything, a man, who evidently had been waiting for us inside, came to the door and gave us a friendly wave, then moved down the steps and started walking toward us. I kept the headlights on so I could see him as he came closer. I got out of the car.

He walked slowly toward us, as if he were carrying some invisible weight, leaning forward and shielding his eyes from the glare of the headlights. He stopped in front of me and seemed to be examining my face. There was a long moment of silence. Then he spoke, in a voice that was almost a whisper, "You must be Hal." He paused and took a deep breath, "I'm Douglas Brunson. You've seen me before, but …" He stopped and seemed to be trying to remember, then his face brightened … "I was in my police uniform then."

We shook hands. I turned and looked over to where Claire was still sitting in the dark. "It's okay," I said. "This is the policeman who was Nancy Ebersole's friend. The one in the photograph I showed you."

Claire got out of the car and stood looking at Douglas, who smiled, "You don't have to worry. I'm leaving town tomorrow, and I just wanted to meet Hal, and thank him before I left."

"Thank me for what?"

"Nancy was always grateful for what you did years ago when Leon attacked her. It was all hushed up and she never got a chance to thank you in person. I told her I would tell you."

"I've always been glad I was there that night. Her mother told me how happy Nancy was at the end, and that you both were very much in love."

Claire came over and stood looking at Douglas. Then without warning she said, "We just saw two people get shot."

Douglas turned very slowly and looked at her. "What happened?"

"The Sheriff said it was all about drugs. It was at the Café Express."

"I'm not surprised. The owner. . ."

"Eddie," Claire said. "His name was Eddie."

Douglas nodded. "Eddie, that's right. He was a dealer and used the Café for a money drop."

"How did you know that," Claire asked.

He leaned forward toward Claire and said in his whispery voice, as if explaining to a child, "Most of the people in North know that."

"Well, Jimmy Spitz shot Eddie, and then the Sheriff shot Jimmy."

Douglas took a step as if to leave, then added, "I have to drive back to Jacksonville tonight."

"We're leaving in the morning, too," Claire said.

Douglas turned back to me, "Nancy loved you, and all your family. She wanted you to know that."

Before I could say anything, Douglas turned and took a couple of slow steps. Claire and I looked at each other and without saying anything we each took one of his arms and walked with him back to his car.

I looked at Claire, who seemed to be coming out of the shocked state she was in after the violence at the Café Express.

"We're so glad you came," Claire said. Nancy must have been a wonderful person."

For the first time Douglas smiled. "Yes, she gave me a reason to keep living."

Douglas opened the car door and slowly eased himself into the seat. The engine started. I could see him pause and look at me. The window rolled down. He put his head out and said "Forget about your mother and the Ebersoles and Leon. There's nothing here now. It's all gone."

Our eyes met for just an instant and I said, "Then tell me what is here?"

"You know the answer to that already. Take her and make a life for yourselves somewhere else. Love is all that matters. Don't throw it away."

The window went up and the car circled around the yard then moved down the driveway and out onto the blacktop, leaving the two of us standing in the dark, following tail lights until they disappeared.

Claire looked at me and said, "He's a good man."

"I think so, too."

Claire took my arm and in her old bravado voice said, "Well, at least he didn't shoot us."

We started walking slowly back toward the house. I knew that all that had happened at the Café Express was driving us away from North; the obsessive questions that would be coming from powerful people who could remain hidden, sending out people to ask about what we had just seen at the Café Express, or to probing into Leon's murder, trying to find out how much we knew. Then again, I thought, perhaps there would be no questions asked. Perhaps the people involved, whoever they were, didn't want any questions asked and it would all be hushed up. And, as much as I wanted to believe him, I didn't completely trust Douglas, who, after talking with Irene Ebersole, might have stopped by to find out if we would be leaving anytime soon.

I turned to Claire. "I have a bottle of whiskey in the pantry. Let's have a drink and talk about what we need to do in the morning. That is, if you are still serious about leaving."

"Try and stop me."

I looked at Claire again, and could tell that the excitement from meeting Douglas was wearing off and that the memory of seeing two people killed was coming back. By the time I was pouring her a drink in the kitchen, she was trembling. It took two more drinks and a sleeping pill to get her in bed. I sat beside her until she finally fell asleep.

I wasn't so lucky. I kept going over all that had happened, not just that night at the Café Express but since I had come back to North a week ago. I knew that Claire had been traumatized by the shootings, and that she would need some help getting through it. Not "over" it. You don't get over something like that, I could hear Dr. Cranston say. I knew Clair needed to get out of North and I could help her with that.

As for me, I had finally come to realize that all the reasons I had given myself for coming back home were no longer important. I didn't care anymore who had killed Leon Putnam. I didn't care if my mother had been involved—in fact, I hoped she had been—and I didn't care who had set Leon's house on fire or what dark violent secrets the Ebersoles had hidden. Besides, it was clear now that nothing I could say or do would change anything. And based on what we saw earlier, with two drug dealers being erased, it now seemed more likely that Leon was killed by drug kingpins in Tallahassee than by a small group of women seeking vengeance for an assault on a girl by a filthy old man that happened twenty years ago. Maybe what Sarah Ebersole hinted at that night after the fire was just wishful thinking, and that they had wanted to kill Leon but that they were glad someone else had done the dirty work for them.

All of this seemed to come together in my mind, leaving me with a clear resolve to let Jess settle up our mother's estate in North while I left tomorrow with Claire. I began roaming around the house looking for things I might have missed, and I finally ended up, where else, sitting at the desk where I first found the photograph taken in Palatka, the one with Leon on the platform with Douglas Brunson standing off to one side and Sarah Ebersole and my mother standing in the crowd. As I mechanically pulled out drawers, I heard a slight rattle from deep inside the desk. I waited for a moment and then pulled out the bottom drawer. It looked empty so I reached back as far as I could reach and could feel a small box. Inside the box, it turned out, was a cell phone, a fairly new Apple iPhone. Taped to the back of the box was what I hoped was the password and phone number. I keyed this in and waited for a few moments and watched as I was connected. The usual icons appeared and I tapped an icon thinking this might be the quickest way to get some information about why my mother, of all people, would be using a cell phone. Surely, I thought, she would have called me on what was clearly her phone, since the welcoming message said "Hello from

Ace," a nickname my father gave her, though neither one of
them would ever say why.

I stared blankly at the screen for a moment, and then
put the phone down on the desk. Of course, I reasoned, everyone has a cell phone now, especially old ladies who want to
keep up with their friends.

I started looking at the most recent correspondence,
which showed that many of "Ace's" friends were not aware
of her death. In fact, there were several wishes for her most
recent birthday. As I continued reading, the messages created
the eerie impression that my mother was still alive.

As I read the messages backwards from the most recent to those that were earlier and earlier, I felt like I was
traveling back in time. Many of the names mentioned were
unknown to me, as I expected, but then, when I reached a
point about two months before my arrival in North, I started
finding messages from the Ebersoles asking first about my
mother's health and then telling her not to worry, and that
"It was going to happen," and then, earlier, asking more and
more often about "When was the best time to do it?" and
ending with admonishments about "Staying strong," and
"Let's follow the plan."

As I read these messages from the Ebersoles to my
mother I had the clear sensation of the ground slowly sliding out from under me. In just the few moments it took me
to read these messages everything I had felt so sure about
before I started reading them—like the drug cartel hit man
killing Leon—all of this was now reversed. Here, I thought,
was clear evidence of the Ebersoles and my mother planning
to murder Leon. Probably it wouldn't stand up in court, since
Leon's name was never mentioned, but I knew what the messages meant. And I remembered Douglas's warning that the
thugs in Tallahassee were after him, but he had not said they

were after the Ebersoles, suggesting that Leon's death was not a drug murder, not what the drug cartel people in Tallahassee were concerned about.

I could only guess about what drug deals might have gone wrong, how much money was owed him, and the years of Leon's keeping secret records on it all. At any rate, I was, in some way, back at the beginning, and that while I had a lot more information about what might have happened, I still lacked certain proof about anything.

I woke up the next morning with my head clear. I just needed to talk to Claire and reassure her about writing her article.

I was thinking about all the things I had to do before leaving when Claire came in and sat down. She put her cell phone down beside her while I poured her a cup of coffee. She gave me an angry, defiant look and said, "I'm dead meat."

I started to say something like "wait a minute" but then thought better of it and just said, "What happened?"

"My editor, Roger" . . . Claire's voice trailed off.

"Roger Bourne?" I queried.

"Yes, Roger the Dodger, who just tweeted me saying I had to be back in Boston and have a story ready within a week or I would no longer be working at his newspaper."

I could tell that talking to Roger had sucked all of that newfound confidence out of her, so I tried to stay casual and just said, "No big deal. You can handle it."

Claire gave me a look like "Am I talking to a crazy man?"

I did not back off, and just said, "Didn't you say last night, after leaving the Café Express that your story just wrote itself? What more do you need? Bang, Bang."

"You mean Bang, Eddie the waiter, and then Bang, Jimmie the drug dealer?"

"Right, and of all this happening after Leon's death and how North and probably all of Florida is in an uproar just days after Leon was buried in his above ground grave, and that, on top of everything else, Leon's house burned down the day after his funeral. What more could an editor want?"

Claire looked at me. "So? . . ." she queried. "Are you still going with me?"

I paused for a moment and then said, "No, I don't think so."

Claire gave me a little crooked smile and turned her head away. "Is that goodbye?"

"No," I said quickly, "Never goodbye. I want to give you a week to finish your story and then I'll fly up to New York to check in at work, then meet you at Logan. Besides, I need to tie up some loose ends here in North and this will give me time to do it."

Claire nodded her head. "Sheriff Moses?"

"Right, Sheriff Moses is one thing. We have to stop by his office and write our statements about what happened last night at the Café Express. We can take separate cars and you can head for Boston when we finish. It won't take long."

"And the other things? Claire asked.

"Jess and I need to put mother's estate in probate and agree on what to do about her house."

"Do you want it?"

"No, and I don't think Jess does either. So, unless her will says otherwise, we'll probably put it up for sale."

Claire gave me a quiet but happy look, and said, "Thanks for doing this. When I came in and sat down, I wasn't sure if I could drive back to Boston and face Roger by myself."

"You've got the upper hand. Just tell Roger you have a great story and that he's lucky to have you, which he is."

We drank our coffee and then Claire stood up, took a deep breath and said, "I'll start putting my things in the car."

I held up my hand and said "There is one more thing."

Claire sat back down. I had been thinking all through our conversation, about finding the cell phone in mother's desk and whether or not I should tell Claire about what was on it and what I thought it meant. I decided this was as good a time as any.

She listened as I explained about finding the cell phone and listening to some of the conversations on Facebook, and how I had interpreted them as pretty much a confirmation of what I had suspected: that the Ebersole sisters had killed Leon, and that my mother was part of it until she became too ill.

To her credit, Claire took it in, and when I had finished, she simply said, "Well, now you know. Your mother was part of it. Isn't that what you've been avoiding all along?" She paused, and then said, "How are you going to deal with it?"

"Right now, unless something happens to change my mind, I'll just take the phone over to Sarah Ebersoles house and tell her what's on it, and advise her to take it out to the middle of the lake and drop it in."

Claire looked at me. "Do it!" she said quietly. Then she pushed away from the table and stood up. "I'm putting my clothes in the car." She turned away, then stopped and said, "By the way, your advice to the Ebersoles won't be in my story."

I sat at the kitchen table watching her go, thinking that it was all too easy. There were too many loose ends surrounding Leon's death, too many people involved with too many motives floating around for wanting to kill him. I should have told Claire to be careful, but, I thought, that would only have thrown her back into the state she was in when she came down for a cup of coffee, with no confidence and afraid to go back to Boston and finish her story for Roger Bourne. It was easy to tell the Ebersoles they should just drop the cell phone in the lake, but I should have reminded Claire that we might be making ourselves accessories to a murder. As the old cliché goes, I felt an ominous foreboding of impending disaster.

While Claire was packing, I called Jess and told him what had gone down at the Café, and it turned out he already knew about it, but he was shocked to learn that Claire and I had seen it all happen. I told him that Claire was leaving for Boston to finish her article for her paper, and that I would be staying to help close up the house and find out what Mother's will had to say. We agreed to meet later in the day.

By the time Claire had finished loading her car, I had stopped agonizing over things I couldn't change and we headed out to tie up all the loose strands so Claire could leave.

Claire needed to check out of her motel and tell the rental car people that she was driving her car back to Boston and that she would turn it in there. Finally, we had to talk to Sheriff Moses and tell him we were leaving. My guess was that we would have to make a sworn statement about the shootings, and that Sheriff Moses would be glad to see us leave.

All was going well until we walked into the Sheriff's office. We were greeted by Sheriff Moses himself and seated at a table to write out and sign our statements. I told him we were leaving right away, and he looked relieved to hear it. He paused, and said, "Don't worry about that other statement about the fire you were going to give me. I have enough to go on."

"Of course, I understand," I said, trying to keep it simple.

Sheriff Moses nodded, and we turned to leave. Then

he said, "Oh, by the way, did you ever meet a man named Douglas Brunson?"

I could feel Claire's hand squeezing my arm tighter and tighter. "Well, yes." I tried to sound relaxed. "Wasn't he the state trooper at Leon's funeral?"

Sheriff Moses lifted his head as if sniffing the air. "How did you know his name?"

I coughed, as if I couldn't remember, and said, "I think Laurel told me. He was at Leon's house just before the funeral. You remember. The divers were there and you left me to watch out for things until they finished diving for whatever had been used to kill Leon. He was standing on the porch."

Claire gave the Sheriff a big smile and said, "Can I use the restroom, Sheriff?"

He pointed and said, "Down the hallway."

"I'll be waiting outside," I called after her. I shook the Sheriff's hand and thanked him for being so understanding, then I turned and walked casually toward the door. A few minutes later Claire came out.

"That was brilliant about Trooper Brunson. Thank God it satisfied the sheriff."

We looked at each other. I could see her start to tremble and I pulled her close. "It's just a week," I said. She pushed away, and nodded.

"Don't try to drive through. Stop in Virginia at a good motel. Eat something besides potato chips, take a shower and go to sleep."

She smiled and said, "I promise," then winked.

I suddenly realized it would take all the self-control I could muster to not beg her to stay—just a few more hours—just another day. I tried to think of something that might work, but all I could think of was to insanely ask, "Can you change a tire?"

Claire got in the car and started the engine. She smiled and said, "Don't worry, I'll call you from Boston."

Her car turned north onto the highway and I yelled, "Call me tonight!" As she pulled away, I could see through the rear window that she was waving goodbye.

EIGHTEEN

Boxes in the Attic

I watched Claire's car until it disappeared in the haze of the hot white cement of a Florida road, then, without thinking I started driving back toward home, but about halfway there I decided on a visit with Laurel and Jess. Laurel wasn't there, but I found Jess sitting upstairs in the attic. He yelled for me to come on up, and I found him surrounded by rows of cardboard boxes.

He gave me a quick smile and said, "Just help me move this box and we can go down and have a few ice-cold beers."

I held up a finger and said, "Just one."

We climbed down the rickety drop-down ladder and went into the kitchen. Jess gave me a questioning look as he filled my glass and pushed it across the table toward me. I waited for the foam to subside, then we both smiled at each other at the same time and took a long swallow out of the frosty glasses.

"So, how did it go with Claire?"

"Better than I expected. I think she was starting to worry about her job and was ready to leave."

"What about you?" Jess turned and gave me the kind of straight-on look I hadn't seen in a long time.

"I'm ready to leave, too."

"No chance in moving back then?"

"None," I said, trying to sound more definite than I felt.

There was a moment of silence as we both studied our half-full glasses. I waited a minute and then decided to ask a question I had been meaning to ask since I came home. "I guess you and Laurel will be staying here?"

"I expect so," Jess said, a little too quickly, "though I'm not really sure why."

"Is that Laurel talking or you?"

"No, it's really both of us," Jess said, "though I'm not really sure why we feel that way."

"No big wedding being planned?"

Jess gave me an "I can't believe you said that" look and said, "What do you think?"

"Of course, no big wedding," I answered.

We sat in silence for a moment. Jess stood up, popped two more bottles and sat back down again. I could tell that he did not want to talk anymore about what he and Laurel were planning for the future, and I didn't feel any need to ask, since his short reply told me a lot. I didn't really want to know about their future plans, but for me it opened up a new window into the past. We all knew that Leon had threatened

Jess and forced him to leave North. But how much of this did Laurel know? Did Laurel ever find out about that night when Leon tried to rape Nancy Ebersole? And why did Laurel leave her job at the University and come back home to work for her father?

Sitting at the table with Jess, I found myself in one of our old family dilemmas; we never talked to each other if we could possibly avoid it. I wasn't so sure about my father, but my mother really never communicated anything to anybody except when someone asked her a direct question, and even then, her answers would be minimal and often baffling. As far as Jess and I knew she never wrote a single letter, not even a Christmas card, to anyone. She was a good listener, and at family dinners, with two or three invited cousins or aunts, she would listen attentively in a sympathetic way, but would offer no opinions or advice. This silence was usually mistaken for understanding and had the effect of allowing others to continue talking, which mother clearly knew was what most people wanted anyway. The only exception to this rule was with my father. At night, after supper, my mother would clear away the dishes and pour a final cup of coffee. My father would light up a cigarette and hand it to my mother and then light up his own, and they would both begin talking in low tones so that if Jess and I were in the living room, we couldn't hear what they were saying.

Jess and I learned at an early age that it was best to be silent and listen and never to ask any embarrassing questions. Only when forced by circumstances would my mother assert herself and take action. For me, the icon of what my mother was capable of remained the knife she left quivering in the wall after Jess had thrown it at me across the kitchen table, and watching the warm grits that she poured over his head slowly stream down his face. So now, looking at Jess across the table as we drank our beer, I understood that the sharpness of Jess's response to my question about a possible wedding was a signal not to go any further. In our family, it wasn't done.

So I waited a moment and then veered away toward what I thought might be a safer topic. "Jesus!" I said, "What are you and Laurel going to do with all those boxes upstairs in the attic?"

"I wish I knew." Jess was silent for a moment and then exclaimed, "I wish to God the fire had burned them all."

"So they were Leon's?"

Jess nodded his head. "That old man saved everything. It will take months to sort it all out."

Jess stood up to get us another beer and I sat there trying to fit together these new pieces to the puzzle. So Leon died, I thought, and then a few days later he was buried. The night of his funeral his house burned down, which meant that Jess and Laurel had started moving things out of Leon's house before he died. Why the rush? Did they set the fire? Did the Ebersoles set the fire? Or did the drug dealers want him out of the way? Or did someone in the state government know what Leon had stashed away at home?

Jess came back and slid another beer across the table. "So what have you been up to?"

I shrugged and said, "Not much."

Jess sat down. "So, what should we do with Mom and Dad's house?"

"See a realtor, I guess, unless you want it."

"No, but I can try to sell it. Do the stove and refrigerator still work?"

"Yes, and there is an old washer and dryer and some furniture that nobody will want to pay for."

"I take it that you're leaving soon?"

"Tomorrow or the next day. What about Mom's old car?"

Jess shrugged. "I can always find somebody who wants an old car with low mileage."

I thought about Jess's answers, which came easily to him and seemed to imply that he was closer in touch with things in North than I had realized. Even though he had moved away, married, and divorced, he must've been secretly coming back to see Laurel, and then it dawned on me that Laurel's leaving her job at the University and moving back to North to help Leon coincided, more or less, with Jess's divorce. And what about Mom? Did she ever say anything to Jess about Nancy and the Ebersoles?

Suddenly, I realized that Jess was looking at me and waiting for some kind of response. "Sorry," I said, "I was just wondering if there was anything else I could do to help you?"

Jess seemed to relax. "No, I can take care of it. There is one thing you should know. Laurel found the old deed for the sale of our land to Leon. She wanted us to have it. It would be easier to sell the house if we sold the land to go with it, if that's okay with you?"

I tried hard not to say it, but all I could think of to say was, "That's amazing."

Jess just smiled and shook his head in agreement. "It really is."

"When did all of this happen?"

"A couple of days before Leon's funeral. Laurel was trying to find some official papers that the state wanted and ran across the deed."

"And that was just a few days after Mom was buried?"

"Yes."

"I should have been there."

"That's partly my fault," Jess said. "I really thought

Mom was going to make it and that I could give you a few extra days to stay in New York and finish up your business. Anyway, it's all over now."

"Maybe," I said. "I'm not sure Sheriff Moses thinks that it's all over, at least not the part about the fire." I wanted to add "and what about who killed Leon?" but backed off, not wanting to bring it up unless Jess mentioned it.

"I think Sheriff Moses and Laurel will work it out," Jess said, giving me another warning look.

"I hope so," I said, "since he seems to think that I might be a suspect."

"Why?"

"Sarah Ebersole says I was the first person to arrive at the scene of the fire."

"Did he tell you not to leave town?"

"Not yet."

"Then leave today," Jess said. "Tomorrow at the latest. Laurel will talk to him about it."

"Why Laurel?" I said.

"It's her house," Jess said, "and Sheriff Moses has already talked to her about it."

"You mean about me?"

"Well, he did indirectly. He asked her if she had any reason to suspect anyone and he mentioned your name since you were the first one there at the fire. Of course she told him the truth, that she was sure you were not involved, for lots of reasons."

"Like what?" I said.

"Like you were having dinner with her and other guests the evening of the fire and you only left her house at about the same time the fire must've started. Not to mention the fact you had been away from North for ten years and had no earthly reason to set Leon's house on fire. Jess leaned back and looked at me. "So stop worrying. It's taken care of."

Laurel must've come in the back door, for she was suddenly standing there looking at us at the entrance to the hallway that led back to the kitchen. Her gray skirt and white blouse made me think she was straight out of a business meeting. She gave us a little wave and a hello in a subdued voice that said, "I'm really tired." She came over and gave Jess a kiss on the cheek and sat down at the table.

I was guessing it had been a meeting with lawyers and I wasn't far off. It turned out that she was involved in a gruesome local case where a friend of hers had been attacked in the hallway of her apartment building by two attack dogs owned by a local power couple that was new in town. The Chessmens were both lawyers who made a living chasing ambulances and getting rich fraternity boys at the University out of trouble.

Laurel's friend, Angela, encountered the two dogs in the hallway, with the Chessmens nowhere in sight. Angela gave a little scream and tried to make it back to her apartment door, but the two dogs, Lucifer and Lucille, caught up with her as she was reaching for her key and by the time they finished Angela had multiple wounds and almost all of her clothes stripped off her body. The Chessmens claimed that Angela's scream had frightened the dogs and that if she had not run away, the dogs would not have attacked.

The trial had been long-delayed since the wily Chessmens had filed multiple countersuits, so that by the time the trial began, Angela's wounds had almost healed, and while multiple photographs had been taken by the police, they did not have the same impact as a healthy Angela sitting in the witness box with no visible wounds showing. Laurel felt that while Angela would win her suit, the amount awarded would be much lower than had the trial taken place right away.

I thought this was the end of the story, but when Jess asked about finding the deed the Chessmens were demanding, I sensed there was more coming. I was right. It seems that the Chessmens were also heavily into speculating on local real estate, and while the highway through town was still just a straight line with no major intersections, the property values around the many lakes in the county had zoomed out of sight.

The Chessmens were trying to locate the deed to five acres of valuable Lakeside property that had gone into escrow when the last owner had died, leaving the deed unfound. "The Chessmens," Laurel said, "had become convinced that Leon had somehow bought the land years ago and allowed the old man to stay there as a kind of caretaker."

"Leon did that a lot," Jess added. He would hold the deed, waiting for the value of the land to go up, and he could get a better deal."

"So it's time to go through all those boxes?"

Laurel sat there with a hopeless look on her face, then waved her hand in a "what can I do" gesture. "You might say Daddy was a hoarder."

"I don't mean to offend," I continued, "but isn't hiding documents like a deed illegal?"

"You betcha!" Laurel answered, "and I've been trying to locate all of Daddy's business dealings ever since I came home. And maybe that deed is in one of those boxes up in the attic, or maybe it was recorded somewhere else under another name, through a legal firm I don't know anything about."

"How are the Chessmens taking all of this?"

"Not well," Laurel said.

"They want a court order to take control of Leon's property," Jess said.

"They're just trying to divert attention away from their killer dogs," Laurel explained. "I'm not sure how to feel.

Sometimes I want to throw my hands up and say to the whole town go ahead and have a look."

Jess leaned forward with an intent look on his face. "Probably this sounds crazy to you, but I honestly think that the Chessmens, or people like the Chessmens, might've had Leon murdered."

For a moment, my head seemed to explode and hoping they didn't notice, I pushed up against the back of the chair to steady myself, and taking a few deep breaths to clear my head. This was the closest I had come to an alternative explanation about Leon's death. On the one hand, I wanted the suggestion about the Chessmens, so that the Ebersoles and my mother could be cleared of any involvement with Leon's death. On the other hand, I could still hear Sarah Ebersole all but admitting that they had killed Leon. And what was making my head spin was the pressure from keeping myself from saying that actually, I was almost certain that the Ebersoles had carried out the murder as a final reckoning with Leon for trying to rape Nancy.

But I didn't say that. Instead, I looked at Jess and then at Laurel and said, "That's really interesting."

Laurel gave me a disgusted look and said, "Is that all you can say?"

That is exactly what I wanted, an invitation to keep talking about what happened to her father, but I didn't want to press it, I wanted it to sound natural. "I just didn't want to upset you by talking about something that might be off limits," trying to sound apologetic. "Did the Ebersoles ever say anything about ..." There was a pause, and Laurel continued with the thought.

"You mean the night Daddy was killed?"

"That's a good place to start. I never heard anybody give any details about what happened that night. Did anybody see anything, or hear a noise?"

"We've never been able to understand it!" Jess exploded. "Irene and her sister Joyce were both supposed to be watching the house."

"Which makes me think that it could not be people like the Chessmens," I said. "It would have to be somebody local, somebody who could figure out the schedule you had for Leon and not draw any attention to himself."

"Or herself," Jess added.

"I just can't believe that Irene and Joyce had anything to do with it," Laurel said, looking hard at Jess. "It's too obvious, and besides, they would be the first suspects."

"Is there anything in their history with Leon that we don't know about? Any old grudges?" I asked. I waited, hoping that something might make Laurel remember things that had been put away for a long time.

Laurel looked thoughtfully at the floor for a moment and then shook her head, "No, not really," then she added as a kind of afterthought, "I mean, it can't be the Ebersoles. We've all known each other forever."

I watched Laurel carefully as she spoke, and I could see no concealment in her face, just puzzlement at a mystery she couldn't solve. But for me, her confusion was my recognition that, without knowing it, she was drawing the net tighter and tighter around the Ebersoles, and probably my mother.

I waited for a moment, unable to believe that the conversation had been allowed to go this far. Then, still trying to sound casual, I moved in another direction. "What about the fire?" I asked. "Do you think the fire was related to Leon's murder in some way?"

Jess and Laurel looked at each other for a moment, then Jess said, "We both think it was, but not in the way you mean."

"How is that?" I asked.

"I mean, we both think that the fire is related to Leon's murder, but we believe that whoever killed Leon did not set the fire."

"So how is it related?" I asked.

Laurel held up her hand, looking at Jess and said "We think that whoever set the fire was trying to hide something, we just don't know what it is, and we think that whoever it is didn't know that Jess and I had moved all of Leon's papers out of his house and into my attic, and that we are really worried that when they find out that Daddy's papers weren't destroyed in the fire, they are going to be dangerously enraged."

"The two crimes, the murder and the fire, just don't go together," Jess interjected. "The person who set the fire was trying to keep something from happening in the future. The murderer was taking revenge for something that happened in the past."

Laurel stood up. "I've got some really good country ham in the fridge. How about a ham sandwich with some potato chips?" Jess and I both nodded, and Laurel looked at Jess. "And maybe a few more bottles of cold beer."

"Sounds good," Jess said, standing up.

I watched them disappear toward the kitchen, and I sat there trying to put together my conversation with Jess and Laurel, and what, I thought, seemed to make more and more sense about Leon's murder and the fire.

I was almost convinced by Laurel, not in what she said about why Leon was murdered, but the way she made me believe that she never knew anything about that night when Leon tried to rape Nancy Ebersole, when, at her graduation party, Nancy stumbled back down the dock toward the group around the fire. It wasn't Laurel who noticed that something was wrong and came rushing down to help Nancy, but another friend who saw that Nancy was in trouble, whose name I never knew and to this day someone I have never asked about.

Jess, of course, was in his usual mode of I've got to protect Laurel, plus he was under a lot of pressure not to reveal too much to Laurel about what I suspected, that our mother and the Ebersoles had either killed Leon or had arranged for someone else to do it, while at the same time he could continue supporting Laurel without revealing what I suspected about Leon's murder. I knew that if Jess were forced to choose, he would always take Laurel's side.

I was fine with that. What I wanted was to get out of North with Jess and Laurel happy. If the situation changed after I left, then Jess and Laurel would have to deal with it. As all of this went through my mind, Laurel came in with a plate of ham sandwiches and potato chips.

"Jess is right behind me with a cooler of beer," Laurel said. She gave me a big smile and placed the platter on the table. I watched her as she arranged some small plates in front of us with calm and graceful movements, and for the first time since I came back I felt relaxed around her, and began to feel more sure about what I was going to do—that is, leave North just as soon as I could.

Laurel gave me a direct look and said "What do you hear from Claire? Are things going okay with her job?"

"She's got a big meeting coming up with her boss, but she seems to think he likes her approach to the story."

There was a pause and I tried to decide which way I wanted the conversation to go. I knew that Laurel and Jess were really asking when I would be leaving, but I wasn't really ready to go there. Instead, I wanted to follow up on the Chessmens, and so I said, "I think I know what the Chessmens were looking for." Jess's eyes widened and he leaned forward with an intense stare and said, "Really!"

"Yes, really. And you will never guess where."

"Tell me," Jess said.

"Remember years ago when Daddy started a new grove of oranges at the side of the swamp where we used to go coon hunting? Well, a small part of that land runs around the swamp and is connected to a lake on the other side."

Jess cocked his head for a moment, then gave me an ahh! hah! look, then turned to Laurel. "That's what the Chessmens are after. The deed for that land is probably in a box upstairs in the attic." Jess paused, as if starting to say something else, then stopped, not wanting to say what we all knew, that Leon got the deed when he foreclosed on us.

"More than likely," Laurel said. "I don't ever recall hearing about it. But then, who knows?" Laurel paused, "So, how do the Chessmens fit into all of this?"

I smiled at Jess. "It all started with Mutt Cox."

Jess wasn't surprised. "I told him to stop by and see if you needed to have some junk carted away."

"But that's not why he came. He wanted me to go with him to meet some people who were asking questions about you," I answered.

"That could only be a few people. I haven't been home that long." Jess paused and looked at Laurel, who bent her head sideways and gave me a suspicious look. "What does this have to do with the Chessmens?"

I could tell she had an idea about where I was going. "They wanted me to ask Jess if you," … I nodded toward Laurel … "had found the deed to the property they were interested in."

Laurel raised her arm and made a fist. "I knew it!"

I thought that this was a good time to leave. "Another mystery solved," I said, and stood up.

Back home, after a quick shower, I walked down to the lake. The old aluminum chair my mother would sit in was still there, folded up against a tree. I looked around, thinking that something was missing, something I didn't do or had not connected with. I thought of the countless times Jess and I had stood here, looking out at the lake just before giving a yell and then jumping in the water, or maybe bringing our rods and reels to go fishing. I remembered the names of the lures we used, and how, when my grandfather taught them to us, they took on a magical quality as he told us where he was on the lake when he caught a big one with a Hula Popper or a Crazy Crawler.

I had stopped fishing a long time ago, and now, standing here by the lake I once knew by heart, I couldn't even remember the last time I had been out looking for bass, with the outboard motor humming and Jess sitting in the bow, his hat brim pushed back by the wind and pointing toward shore, where, in a likely cove he knew about, the big lunkers were waiting.

NINETEEN

The Girl in a Red Sox Cap

anging on the wall behind his desk, Dr. Cranston had a framed drawing of the Buddha meditating beneath a tree. At the bottom of the picture were these words:

> *What is time but loss? What is thought but pain?*
>
> *The Buddha sits beneath his tree, he doesn't mind the rain.*

I had always meant to ask him why he had this particular, somewhat discouraging sign posted behind him for all of his patients to see. Naturally, given my family history of never communicating anything personal to anybody except at gunpoint, I never got around to asking him about it, though I often felt it was strange for a doctor practicing what some people call "the talking cure," to have that sign as what you might call an unofficial motto. At least that is the way I usually interpreted it.

But now, in North, where I was surrounded by the wreckage, as they say, that time hath wrought, and feeling the pain brought about by the recognition that I, too, was involved in creating much of the mess I had uncovered, it now seems to me that Dr. Cranston's sign pretty much says it all. My parents, after they lost the orange groves and most of their land, stayed in North and ended up losing almost everything. Why did that one moment where, as a boy, I watched Leon attacking Nancy Ebersole, seem to define everything that would happen later?

All of this was running through my mind as I began what I hoped was my final tour around the house. Without noticing it, I had started mentally cataloging everything, and of course this memory led me back to Claire, so I sent her a quick message saying I was on my way and then sent a different one to my crew at work in New York.

I finished my coffee and looked around, snapped the latches and lugged the suitcase out to the car. I had been planning to take some pictures of the house and grounds and so I pulled out my cell phone again and ambled around to view the house from different angles.

It was Wednesday, and as I drove to the airport, I tried to stay focused by concentrating on one small thing at a time. The JAX terminal was crowded. I dropped off my rental car and checked in my luggage. I bought a newspaper and a mystery novel, then came the necessary cup of coffee and a trip to the men's room. By the time I boarded the jet I was ready to leave Florida and those last agonizing weeks behind, but we were delayed by a quick moving rainstorm coming in unexpectedly off the Atlantic, with gusty winds blowing wildly from different directions. Fortunately, the storm disappeared as fast as it came, and after a brief delay, we were allowed to lift off. Soon after takeoff, we left the Sunshine State behind as the pilot said over the loudspeaker, "Welcome to Georgia." We stopped in Atlanta but did not have to change planes, and I settled in for the long flight to La Guardia. It was sunshine all the way.

As the flight settled in to routine, I watched the landscape below and thought about what was waiting for me in New York. Before leaving for the airport I had called Claire in Boston to let her know my schedule. My flight was leaving on time and I would arrive at La Guardia about one, Wednesday afternoon. I needed to check in at my office and then head over to my apartment. Thursday I had an appointment with Dr. Cranston and then what I hoped would be a full day back at work. Unless things had changed Claire would leave Boston late Friday and I would pick her up at the airport. I told her that I loved her and that I wanted us to get married and live together forever. Her only response was a question, "How were things in North when you left?"

All I could think of to say was, "It's over."

There was a pause and then Claire asked, "Over as in people are going to jail or over because nobody gives a damn."

"Over because, at least for now, nobody is going to jail and over because I don't give a damn anymore."

"Oh," was all Claire said, so I hurried on. "How did things go with Roger?"

"I still have a job," Claire said, with no hint in her voice of whether this was good or bad.

I took that as a positive response and said, "That's encouraging news."

"How is that so encouraging?" Claire asked.

"Because you have an option now. You can stay at the paper or resign. It's up to you."

All Claire said was a long, drawn out, "Reaaally? I never thought of that."

Realizing this wasn't going well, I changed direction. "How about sushi Friday night?"

"That would be nice. Oh, and my plane gets in at 7 o'clock. I'm on American, Gate 3."

"Great," was all I could manage. I waited, hoping she would say more but there was only silence, so I tried to finesse her, not saying much with, "Wear your Red Sox cap so I can spot you over the crowd."

Another pause before Claire answered, coming almost close to sounding happy about our being together. "Oh, sure. I'll be there."

"I love you," I said, in what I hoped was an offhand but sincere voice.

"That's good," Claire replied. "See you Friday at 7. Bye."

I hung up, shaken and trying to assess just how bad the damage was. I needed help, and fortunately I had scheduled a session early afternoon on Thursday with Dr. Cranston, who, when I had called him, let me know that his making room for me would cause him scheduling problems, and that he was doing me a really big favor. I thanked him several times, since I knew that this was true. A few years ago at our first meeting he emphasized how important it was to keep our scheduled appointments. "I'm dealing with crazy people here, so don't cause me any unnecessary worries." His agreeing to see me on short notice was his way of recognizing how difficult the last few weeks in North had been for me, and that he knew I needed to see him.

I needed to talk to Dr. Cranston about Claire, and all

that had happened in North, but not over the phone. Even though her editor had liked it, I felt that my suggesting she could come to North and write about Leon's murder was a big mistake. I sold the idea to Claire as a way to keep her job, but the truth was that I needed Claire in North. At the time, I believed that I couldn't face going home alone. I remembered the surge of unexpected surprise and happiness I felt when sitting alone at the Café Express, I saw her quietly looking at me from across the room.

But for Claire, North turned out to be a place where she constantly was humiliated by the people she tried to interview, who didn't take her seriously as a journalist and was a stranger who was asking dangerous questions. I should have gone with her for her first few interviews, even if it meant sitting in the car while she went inside. Instead, I let the past gradually suck me in. I won't say I was indifferent to Claire's situation, but I was distracted, and by the time she left, after the shootings and the visit from Douglas Brunson, she found herself alone in Boston, writing the story about North for Roger Bourne, and with her job in the balance.

I knew that by placing Claire in North with almost no support from me made her doubt the way I felt about her, and that now, looking back, my not realizing these consequences made her doubt her own sense of what was happening to us. I can remember how I would catch her looking at me in a questioning way, in what I now realize was a signal of her distress, as if she needed support from me, and that she could not even put a name to her fears. It was a silent plea for help that I pushed aside.

In a children's book, a little girl named Rose had feelings similar to Claire's. Rose becomes afraid that her own existence could be lost in the overwhelming vastness of the world, so she carved a statement affirming her name in circular fashion around a tree, linking the end to the beginning so it became never ending: "Rose is a Rose is a Rose is a Rose." This was some comfort to Rose and she gradually grew to be less afraid. Perhaps it was like a Tibetan prayer wheel that the monks keep turning, with its prayers repeated over and over again. But writing about Leon and North proved no comfort for Claire.

My plane landed safely at La Guardia mid-afternoon Wednesday. After the usual baggage hassle and the Uber ride, I found myself unpacking in my apartment and slowly recovering from the effects of that modern magic called jet travel, where you were one moment in a place of murder and lies you once called home, and in the next moment you were back in what seemed to be a haven of reason. I knew of course that it wasn't all that reasonable in the city, but at least it was something I could deal with. Or so I thought until I checked my cell phone and remembered to look at the pictures I took of our house just before I left for the airport.

What I saw was the uncanny. The house was reproduced in all its digital exactness, without the roughness of human focus, and to me, this exactness made it seem unreal, or better, perhaps—the house seemed more real than real, as if it existed in some timeless dimension elsewhere. As I scrolled through the pictures, I had the sinking feeling that no matter how far away from North I travelled, in my mind the house would always be there and that I could never escape.

I was thinking about these things the next day as I found myself climbing the familiar steps that lead to Dr. Cranston's office. After the hellos and his usual quick look of scrutiny to make sure, as he once put it, that I wasn't getting ready to run screaming out the door, I sat down and launched in about my love for Claire and how I felt that I had ruined things with my lack of perception about the consequences for her of coming to North.

He waited until I had finished and then said, "This is the kind of outlook people choose in order to avoid a life filled with disappointment."

"What does that mean?"

"It's the old 'I'm never disappointed because I always expect to be disappointed' routine."

"How can you be so sure?" I asked.

"So sure of what?" he replied.

"About what I really choose to believe as my way of life."

"Why are you here? If I'm wrong, then tell me about it."

"I don't remember consciously choosing 'a disappointing way of life.' That sounds too melodramatic."

"So it just happens for no reason, like this?" Dr. Cranston slammed his hand on his desk.

"No, not just like that. Maybe somewhere in between."

Dr. Cranston considered this for a moment, shaking his head back and forth and making a humming sound. "Well, maybe, and maybe not. What about Claire?"

"What about her?"

"You mean there's no plan for your future with her? What do you think about when you think about Claire? Or better, what do you talk about when you try to decide about your future together? I have an idea that Claire isn't just winging it?"

I thought this over. "I don't think she is either. Really, we were just getting to that point when Mom died and I headed back to North, just before Leon was killed."

Dr. Cranston held up a single finger and said "One,"

then added, "but it's going to happen. Can't you envision a great powwow in the near future where the two of you will decide about marriage, your jobs, and where you're going to settle down?"

"Well sure. It's out there, at least in my mind."

"So where do you think it's headed?"

I expected this, the answering a question with a question, but I decided to try for a direct response. "I think you're saying that we should give our lives some direction we can believe in, even if we are wrong?"

Dr. Cranston shook his head back and forth again and said, "No, not really. I'm not a GPS giving directions for you to follow."

I threw my hands up in exasperation. "Well, what is it, really?"

"You don't understand what's troubling you. Probably you never will, directly."

"I'll settle for indirectly."

"Good."

There was a pause. I waited, not knowing what else to do.

Dr. Cranston shifted in his chair, and looking at me, he gave an obviously stagey cough.

I smiled, since I always started coughing at moments like this, and he would invariably say, "Don't cough," meaning something like "Since you can't access what your unconscious is trying to deal with, you cough instead."

"But . . . ," I started to say.

Dr. Cranston immediately held up his hand, giving me a stop sign. This was another one of my defenses, since often at moments like this, I would start almost every sentence with "but," which, he would point out, was an unconscious way of objecting to what we were talking about. It took me months to become aware of it, but (there I go again) I still keep doing it. (This, "I know very well … But I still keep doing it" was a pattern with many variations. Dr. Cranston recommended Shakespeare's sonnets as a master class in this form of self-defense.)

Fighting back, I gave a death-rattle cough and said, "But," I said defensively, "what am I looking for? Is there some kind of sign or signal that tells me how to understand something that you say I can't really understand?"

"You have to look for the small things, those minor moments of discomfort when you don't realize it and are not paying attention. For example, how do you feel when you get ready to come here for one of our delightful sessions?"

I thought about it for a moment and shrugged. "OK, I guess."

I paused, thinking about it and said, "Well, maybe just a little bit of worry about what to say when I get here."

"That's a good place to start," Dr. Cranston said.

"Start with what?"

"That little bit of worry. Did you feel it today?"

"Yes."

"Where were you when you felt it?"

"I was coming out of my apartment and walking toward my car."

"Were you thinking about anything in particular?"

"Uhhh …" I tried to remember. "I was thinking about Claire."

"What does Claire rhyme with?" Dr. Cranston said quickly.

"Chair?" I answered, trying to keep up.

"So, Claire in a chair is a…?" Dr. Cranston asked.

"Scare?" … I said, suppressing an urge to cough.

Dr. Cranston gave me a grim smile. "Good, now try

to connect them."

Memories suddenly came flooding back. "I once told Claire about a game where I arranged furniture in the room to memorize things, and she was worried about something and I was trying to calm her down."

"Without a sound?" Dr. Cranston asked, rhyming again.

I waited, not sure where this was going.

"Who had to be calmed down in your life?"

There was a long, long pause. "My mother," I said. Without realizing it, I had dropped deep down and far back.

Dr. Cranston held up two fingers "Two," then continued with "Why did you have to calm her down?"

"Because she would leave me if I wasn't good."

"So you understood? You had to be good? And, as you said just a few moments ago, when you and Claire were about to be good and be understood by each other, what happened?"

"My mother died."

"Three," he said, again with the fingers.

"And ...?"

"I went back home."

Dr. Cranston did his crazy man imitation, waving his arms as he yelled, "Yikes! He went back home!"

This hit me like a blow, and I wasn't surprised at what he said next.

"So tell me, when did you leave home?"

"After college, I guess?"

"No, no, no. I mean leave for good."

"About three months after I graduated from college, say fifteen years ago."

"And since then how many times have you been back home?"

I knew the answer but didn't want to say it. "I've never been back."

"Imagine that," Dr. Cranston said softly. "Fifteen years and he never went back home …not even to see his mother. And did you ever write to her?"

"No."

"Did she ever write to you?"

I couldn't help but laugh. "My mother never wrote to anybody."

Dr. Cranston, of course, knew most of this history already, but he had never put it all together with more recent issues like Claire and Leon. He looked at his watch. "Time to leave. Go meet Claire at the airport."

I stood up. "Next week?"

"I'm not going anywhere." As I opened the door, Dr. Cranston yelled "Four fingers, one for each time your mother made you feel guilty."

I found my car and headed out toward the expressway to La Guardia. "American Airlines, Gate 3," I kept repeating, "wearing a red beret." It was early, around one o'clock, and Claire's flight wasn't due to land until three but I didn't care; I couldn't face going back to an empty apartment without her. By the time I parked I was almost trembling from anxiety and the pent-up need to be with Claire, to see her, to feel her, to have my arms around her and not take them away. I walked through the check-in rooms and found a table near the enormous windows where you could watch the planes landing and taking off.

A bar was behind me and the waitresses were circulating through the lobby. I ordered a Corona and it came ice cold. That was a good sign, I thought, and with almost two hours still to go, I began playing a game called looking for good signs. How many waitresses could I count in the next ten minutes? How many different airlines would arrive and from how many cities? How many American flights would arrive? Claire's flight, I assumed, was the shuttle from Boston. I started keeping score on a napkin. Nothing helped. I wanted another Corona desperately but then I remembered that I had to drive back to the city. I ordered another Corona anyway and went back to counting. Two security guards strolled by and stopped near my table. They seemed to be deciding something. One of the guards turned and looked at me. I looked away and then I started writing something on my napkin. When I looked up, the guards were gone. Two couples were talking and laughing at another table. How can they be so happy, I thought, at a time like this? I tried to keep writing but my hands wouldn't cooperate. My waitress came up with my second Corona. I started to pay her, but she looked at the money and said, "That's your third." She pointed to the two empty bottles on the table. "See." She looked at me and laughed, in a throaty, knowing way. "What time does she get in?"

"Three," I mumbled. The waitress turned and looked at a big clock hanging behind the bar. "You've got about ten minutes."

I gave the waitress the money for the beers along with a huge tip for good luck. I took a deep breath, then slowly exhaled. After a couple more deep breaths, I leaned back in my chair and let the tension that was torqued up inside me slowly unwind. What happened? Just moments ago it was a few minutes after one. Somehow, without realizing it, I must have blanked out. Then I heard "American Airlines Flight 365 from Boston now arriving at Gate 3."

I stood outside with a small crowd looking down the long connecting tunnel as the passengers on Claire's flight started to appear, at first in just a few dribbles, and then a flood. This was the Friday afternoon shuttle and most of the passengers were all wearing the same grey or blue corporate business suits and commuting back home after long meetings in the Boston office. I stood on my toes looking for a baseball cap. After a few minutes I could see Claire's cap bobbing along, getting closer until I could see her face. I waved and waved. She caught sight of me, gave me a big smile and waved back. Then she was in my arms, and looking up at me with the 'It's your move, big shot' kind of dare in her eyes that I loved.

We pulled away. I looked at her and her confidence faded, and she seemed to be looking back at me now with just a touch of questioning darkness in her eyes. Then there was a flicker and it was gone. Arm in arm we took the escalator down to retrieve her bag and then hurried to the car. We drove in silence for a few miles with Claire's head on my shoulder.

"How did you leave things at the paper?" I asked.

"The paper is fine. I'm doing the local art galleries and museum shows, which I like."

"And…?" I queried, sensing something else was coming.

"Well, I've decided I don't want to make a career out of journalism. There's nothing wrong with it, but it's just not for me."

"Have you talked to Roger about it?"

"No, not yet. I'll wait till I've looked at a few more things."

"But you are leaning toward something?"

"I suppose." Another pause. "I really do like the art world."

I didn't want to push her, so I just added, "It's worth a try."

We drove on in silence, content to just be with each other after the long separation. I knew the route back to the city by heart, so I relaxed and thought about what Claire had said and was able to connect two dots; first, Claire was covering the art scene for her paper. Then, I remembered my only visit with Claire to Connecticut for the 'meet her family' visit. There was her father, James (not Jim), a banker, and stuffy until the gin took effect, a nervous mother, Ellen, an older version of Claire with eyes that kept darting back to Jim as he mixed me another martini, and Claire's younger sister Jane, who was delightful, and, though it was never mentioned, was secretly thrilled at the prospect of a wedding. What I gradually became aware of was that the house was filled with Claire's paintings; lovely water colors that were more than just promising, but were the work of someone who could realize her own unique vision of the world in color and space.

Later that night, as Claire and I sat alone in front of a blazing fire, I asked about her art, and said how impressed I was with the paintings I had seen. But when I suggested that she was wasting her time at the paper and instead should think about formal study in a school with a good art department, all she would do was shrug and say in an almost inaudible whisper "I'm just not ready for that."

A parking lot was next to my building where I paid a monthly fee for a reserved space. Claire was still sleeping with her head on my shoulder. Looking at her, I could tell that she was totally relaxed and I thought that with her work at the paper covering the art scene, that maybe she was now confident enough to think about full-time study in a school with a good reputation in the arts. I knew better now not to push her anymore in that direction. She would have to make up her own mind.

My apartment was the basic four room square model,

with a kitchen, the living room/dining room combo, a bedroom and bath. But the rooms were slightly larger than the
standard version, and I had a nice balcony with a decent view.
Each floor was square with four apartments, so I had neighbors, which I didn't mind. I had taken it furnished, not wanting to bother with buying new stuff.

Claire looked around as we entered and said, "This is
nice."

"But not too nice," I said. "I'll find something better
when my lease runs out next year." I pointed out the bathroom and then took Claire's bag into the bedroom. "If you
want to freshen up or shower, go ahead."

Claire brightened up and said, "Yes, I'd like that, if we
have time. For some reason I always feel grubby after flying."

I waited on the balcony for a few minutes, and then
went inside. I sat on the sofa, propped my feet up on an
ottoman and began checking messages. I could hear the
shower running and then stop. Another ten minutes and
Claire came out looking gorgeous, with a beautiful outfit of
jade green slacks, a matching top and white shoes. Before I
could say anything she came over and sat in my lap. Putting
her arms around me, she whispered, "Are you really glad I'm
here?"

For the first time in what seemed like forever we really
kissed for a long, lovely moment, then Claire slowly pushed
away. She nuzzled me with her nose and said, "That was nice,"
and then slipped off my lap. She cocked her head sideways
and said, "Let's take a walk and eat sushi."

Outside, we crossed Madison Square Park and headed toward the East Village. "It's just a couple of blocks," I
said. "Not far at all." It was called China Delight, a not very
original name, but the food was good, and it was one of the
few remaining restaurants where you could actually hear the

person across from you talking, which was why I chose it. I wanted us to take our time, have a long, slow meal, and really talk without having to shout.

We pushed through the usual bamboo curtain into a cavernous room filled with mostly empty tables. The owner and his wife were standing in the back holding menus and waving. Their children, two small girls, came rushing toward us, jumping up and down and shouting what sounded like, "Pray for you! Pray for you!" as they pointed toward the back wall where we could see only a few folded chairs and an old piano.

I wasn't sure what was happening, but Claire caught on, "They want to play for us." Claire nodded, "Yes, yes, we'd love to hear something."

The two girls rushed back to the piano and with both of them sitting on the one bench launched in to a thundering four handed version of *The Star-Spangled Banner*. I wasn't sure how to proceed, but Claire understood, standing rigidly at attention and saluting. I thought, 'Why not?' and solemnly crossed my arm over my chest. An older couple followed, slowly standing up and crossing their arms and we listened all the way through to "*home of the brave*." We all clapped and Claire shouted "Bravo!"

I glanced at my watch. It was almost six o'clock. I seemed to have lost all sense of time. Claire saw me looking and said, "I know, I made us late. It took us almost an hour to secure my bag at the carousel."

I couldn't even remember being at the carousel. All I could do was shrug and say, "I guess so."

We found a table near the front by the windows. We both went vegetarian and ordered California rolls with noodles and miso soup. I didn't want to directly plunge into what I told Dr. Cranston about North and my feeling that I had left

Claire hanging out to dry. So I asked her to bring me up to date on her family.

She smiled. "Well, I did mention that we would probably be getting married this summer. Jane and Mom started to cry, and my dad tried to look serious, but then he actually smiled and told me how pleased he was. Your visit helped a lot. At least they know what you look like. That's my story. I think, however, at least on the surface, I know a lot more about you after spending some time in North. I even met your former wife there. I wonder," Claire continued, "is this a kind of talk about the in-laws' session or is there something else?"

"A little of both, I guess. I want to tell you how much I love you, and that after you left North, I felt as if you had taken a part of me with you. I need you, but strangely enough, it was your absence that made everything clear. It was you supporting me in North, and I didn't give you much in return."

"That's true," Claire said, "and it really hurt. So why did you do it?"

"I became obsessed with finding out the truth about Leon's murder. I thought I had to know who killed Leon and if my mother was involved. Or was it really about Nancy Ebersole? Or money and politics? At the same time, I think I don't really care who was involved. It just doesn't matter."

"Do you have an answer now?" Claire asked. "Did you find something that mattered?"

"I think so. I think it was because of Nancy. I was just a kid, but I was her only witness. I was the one who could have told the truth about that night and what happened to Nancy. I never realized how I felt about any of this until Leon was killed and I came back home."

"But you did tell the truth. Didn't your mother and

Nancy's mother threaten Leon with the truth? Didn't they make him send Nancy something every month?"

"That was just a payoff. It wasn't something public. Nancy deserved more than hush money."

"Anything else?" Claire asked.

"Maybe Nancy was happy at the end; I hope so. I think her mother said that she and Douglas Brunson were very much in love and were going to get married."

The minute I said this I could sense something change in Claire. "You remember, we met him that night, after the …" I paused.

"The shootings," Claire said. "He was waiting for us."

Claire sat there, biting her lip. "What's wrong?" I took her hand.

Claire pulled her hand away and sat back. "I wasn't going to tell you this, at least not tonight. I wanted to wait. But maybe this is the best time. Anyway, you know the newspaper gets a lot of what are called feeds from sources here and overseas. So, I was looking for a story and I came across one with a Jacksonville headline. It said that a former state trooper, Douglas Brunson, had been found dead in a motel room in downtown Jacksonville. His death was an apparent suicide."

"My God," I moaned, "that's…" I had to force myself to keep from throwing up. "It just never ends, does it?"

"Maybe it does," Claire said. "Maybe this is the end."

I laughed. No, it would never be quite the end. But maybe … I suddenly remembered that picture at my mother's house, the one of Leon at the park, getting an award, the one with Sarah Ebersole looking across the crowd at my mother, or at least who I thought was mother.

"It made no sense," I blurted out, "what she wrote on the back."

"What?" Claire asked.

"She wrote it to me, specifically. Something like 'in the land of the law now' or 'in the hands of the law now.' I didn't get it. And there were letters and numbers, maybe a telephone number. I don't know." I was speaking so quickly, I was sure I was hyperventilating. The words were tumbling over each other. I seemed to be almost yelling. "But she must have meant that justice for Leon, whatever that was, was now in the hands of the law—and . . ."

Claire got it. "And the law was the trooper, Doug-. . ."

"Douglas Brunson! Exactly!"

We each paused, if only to let the oxygen catch up.

I started back up, slowly. "Even if it was the last thing he ever. . ."

"Yes, she said. "The last thing."

We sat in silence.

Now it was Claire's turn to take my hand. "Let's go back to your place. We can lie on the sofa and have a glass of good wine. We can talk all night and make plans." She looked at me, waiting for my assent.

"Yes," I said. "Yes."

It had been raining, and we walked through the puddles with a gusty wind blowing down the long canyons of the high buildings. Claire shivered and leaned against me. I put my arms around her and pulled her close. "That's a cold wind," Claire said. She looked up at me and smiled. "I'll bet it's from the north."

TWENTY

Reckonings

I can see now, looking back, why the next few months were not that easy. Claire and I continued to struggle with our separate demons. This was necessary, Dr. Cranston said. We had our moments of despair and this led to anger and hurt feelings. We even tried to break up a couple of times but couldn't make it work, so a year later we got married on the beach below Little Boar's Head, where, long ago, it seems now, I had tried to keep up with Claire as we raced back to Roger Bourne's house. Somehow, saying our marriage vows helped. The Bourne family gave us a lovely breakfast before the wedding and then we all walked down to the beach for the ceremony. Dr. Cranston was there with a girlfriend half his age. Jess was the best man and Laurel was a bridesmaid, along with Claire's younger sister Jane. Claire's father, James, walked with her through the sand and handed her to me. That night James and Ellen rented the state park beach house and we had champagne with our lobsters and a country band played square dance music. Three months later, with Roger's blessing, Claire left the paper and enrolled at NYU to take art lessons. She has a group of small galleries that show her work. We have two children now, a daughter almost six who knows exactly how her parents should behave as she gets ready to enter the first grade, and a son who is two and was born with a motor that never stops. Their names are Nancy and Douglas.

ACKNOWLEDGMENTS

I owe great thanks to Ray McAllister for his careful and intuitive editing and his advice about the book at many stages. My friends and family have helped in ways over the years that have been greater than they have known. They are listed here: Billy, Kitty, Bitsy, Margaret and Lou, Frances, Maria, Rosalind, Anne Beale, Amanda and Jim, Janet and Cameron, Jane. Special long-distance thanks go to Michael Knight, Margaret Archenbault, Catherine Hamilton, and Carrie Brown. I thank the talented authors who offered generous back-cover praise: Andy Straka, Charles Oldham, and the afore-mentioned Michael Knight. Finally, I thank the proofreaders who found points to sharpen and polish: Jane Holland, Sharon Perutelli, Vicki Pepper, Kris Pepper, and Vicki McAllister.

Roy Robbins.

ABOUT THE AUTHOR

ROY ROBBINS is an award-winning playwright and poet. This, his first novel, reflects a fascination with Florida that began when his family moved from upstate South Carolina, a land of red dirt hills and mountains, to a land of hurricanes, ocean and lakes, a strange place where he watched flying coconuts sail past his windows. It is in this Florida of pine woods, swamps and storms that *North* is set.

His training has been eclectic. Robbins studied poetry with James Dickey at the University of South Carolina, theater at the American Academy of Dramatic Arts in New York, and literature at the University of Virginia. He has worked as a waiter, a reporter, a teacher, and a director of institutional research in colleges and universities. He has lived in Bolivia.

Robbins' first play, the full-length *King Momo*, was honored in 1988 at London's International Playwrighting Festival. He followed with a succession of one-act and full-length plays performed and read in New York, Providence, and Charlottesville: *Sudden Improvement, Slow Instructions*, and *Prove That You Love Me*. His poetry has been honored, too— with the Deep South Prize for the Lyric for one—and has been published in *The Southern Poetry Review, The Virginia Literary Journal, The Northeast Journal,* and other publications. In 2015, a book of his poetry, *Poster Art Nights*, was published.

Robbins has conducted readings of his work at galleries and bookstores in Kentucky, North Carolina and Virginia. At Richmond's Hill Gallery, he presented his poems alongside the landscape paintings of artist Lindsay Nolting. In 2018, he was a featured reader at Appalachian State University's celebration of the famed Black Mountain College writers and artists.

Robbins now lives in rural Virginia with his wife, the writer Susan Pepper Robbins, who teaches writing at Hampden-Sydney College.

ROYROBBINS-AUTHOR.COM

Books That Endure

BEACH GLASS
Books

BeachGlassBooks.com